200 HARLEY STREET

Welcome to the luxurious premises of the exclusive Hunter Clinic, world renowned in plastic and reconstructive surgery, set right on Harley Street, the centre of elite clinical excellence, in the heart of London's glittering West End!

Owned by two very different brothers, Leo and Ethan Hunter, the Hunter Clinic undertakes both cosmetic and reconstructive surgery. Playboy Leo handles the rich and famous clients, enjoying the red-carpet glamour of London's A-list social scene, while brooding ex-army doc Ethan focuses his time on his passion—transforming the lives of injured war heroes and civilian casualties of war.

Emotion and drama abound against the backdrop of one of Europe's most glamorous cities, as Leo and Ethan work through their tensions and find women who will change their lives forever!

200 HARLEY STREET

Glamour, intensity, desire—the lives and loves of London's hottest team of surgeons!

Dear Reader,

I love writing continuity stories, as it's a great excuse to work with my fellow authors and bounce ideas around. When my editor suggested this one to me I leaped at the chance. Special thanks to Louisa George, Amy Andrews and Scarlet Wilson for letting me take liberties with their characters, and being so brilliantly accommodating. Thanks to my son, Chris Brooks, for answering questions about military stuff, and to Chris Craig for technical advice about the kind of workouts that Marco could do post-injury.

Becca Anderson and Prince Marco come from completely different worlds. And although there's a lot of attraction between them they also need to learn to trust each other before they can reignite their past love and get their happy ending. I love the way Becca's managed to rise above such an awful past and a total lack of family support—and that she eventually finds the support and the family she deserves in Prince Marco. I also enjoyed giving Marco a tough time; for someone who's used to a life of action, having to wait and let things take their natural course is really, really difficult. And Becca most definitely teaches him patience….

I hope you'll enjoy Marco's fabulous house on the edge of Regent's Park. And the tango at the salsa club (we learned a couple of new steps in the tango at dance class while I was writing this, so it was great to do a bit of personal research!). But most of all I hope you'll enjoy seeing Becca and Marco fall in love all over again, and this time learn to trust each other.

I'm always delighted to hear from readers, so do come and visit me at www.katehardy.com.

With love,

Kate Hardy

200 HARLEY STREET: THE SOLDIER PRINCE

KATE HARDY

HARLEQUIN® MEDICAL ROMANCE™

Recycling programs for this product may not exist in your area.

ISBN-13: 978-0-373-06967-5

200 HARLEY STREET: THE SOLDIER PRINCE

First North American Publication 2014

Special thanks and acknowledgment are given to Kate Hardy for her contribution to the 200 Harley Street series.

This edition published by arrangement with Harlequin Books S.A.

For questions and comments about the quality of this book, please contact us at CustomerService@Harlequin.com.

Printed in U.S.A.

Dedication

For the *200 Harley Street* authors—I loved working with you!

Also, special thanks to Chris Brooks for technical help with military stuff, and to Chris Craig for technical help with workout programmes following injury—much appreciated, guys :)

200 HARLEY STREET

*Glamour, intensity, desire—the lives and loves
of London's hottest team of surgeons!*

**For the next four months enter the world of London's elite surgeons
as they transform the lives of their patients and find love amid
a sea of passions and tensions!**

In April, renowned plastic surgeon and legendary playboy Leo Hunter
can't resist the challenge of unbuttoning the intriguing
new head nurse, Lizzie Birch!
200 HARLEY STREET: SURGEON IN A TUX by Carol Marinelli

And glamorous Head of PR Lexi Robbins is determined to make gruff,
grieving and supersexy Scottish surgeon Iain MacKenzie
her Hunter Clinic star!
*200 HARLEY STREET: GIRL FROM THE RED CARPET
by Scarlet Wilson*

In May, top-notch surgeons and estranged spouses Rafael and
Abbie de Luca find being forced to work together again tough as
their passion is as incendiary as ever!
200 HARLEY STREET: THE PROUD ITALIAN by Alison Roberts

And one night with new colleague surgeon Grace Turner sees former
Hollywood plastic surgeon Mitchell Cooper daring to live again…
*200 HARLEY STREET: AMERICAN SURGEON IN LONDON
by Lynne Marshall*

Then, in June, injured war hero Prince Marco meets physical therapist
Becca Anderson—the woman he once shared a
magical *forbidden* summer romance with long ago…
200 HARLEY STREET: THE SOLDIER PRINCE by Kate Hardy

When genius microsurgeon Edward North meets single mom nurse
Charlotte King she opens his eyes to a whole new world…
200 HARLEY STREET: THE ENIGMATIC SURGEON by Annie Claydon

Finally join us in July, when junior surgeon Kara must work with hot-shot
Irish surgeon Declan Underwood—the man she kissed at the hospital ball!
*200 HARLEY STREET: THE SHAMELESS MAVERICK
by Louisa George*

And brilliant charity surgeon Olivia Fairchild faces the man who once broke
her heart—damaged ex-soldier Ethan Hunter. Yet she's unprepared for his
haunted eyes and the shock of his sensual touch…!
200 HARLEY STREET: THE TORTURED HERO by Amy Andrews

Experience glamour, tension, heartbreak and emotion at

**200 HARLEY STREET in this new eight-book continuity
from Harlequin® Medical Romance™.**

**These books are also available in ebook format
from www.Harlequin.com.**

PROLOGUE

THAT WAS THE last of the men.

Safe.

Or were they? The rescue had been slightly too easy for Marco's liking. The insurgents didn't usually give up that quickly. And this definitely felt like a false sense of security, he thought as he drove the Jeep back towards base.

'Pedro, I need you to keep a close eye out on the way back. Anything that makes you even slightly uneasy, you tell me immediately,' he said to his second-in-command.

'Sir. You're expecting an ambush?'

'Maybe.'

Pedro had worked with him long enough to follow his train of thought. 'You're right. It was a bit too easy. They're prob—'

The word was cut off by a loud boom.

Bomb, Marco thought, and was about to slam on the brakes when the blast wave smashed into the Jeep, cracking the screen. Marco put his left hand up automatically to shield his eyes; even as he did so, he was aware of splintering glass spiking into his skin.

But he didn't have time to worry about the pain. The blast wave had made the Jeep slew. He tried to steer out of the skid, but the blast wave was just too strong and the car rolled.

Everything went into slow motion, and Marco's senses were working overtime. Everything felt magnified. The bang of the rest of the glass imploding, the scrape of metal, the salty, rusty smell of blood.

Finally, they came to a halt. Upside down.

Oh, great.

He knew they were a sitting target in the Jeep. They needed to get out—right now. It would take just one RPG fired into the fuel tank to blow them all sky-high…

Then again, Marco also knew that the insurgents preferred prisoners to dead men. Live prisoners would be much more useful to them. Especially if one of them was second in line to a throne—even if the throne in question was that of a relatively small south European country. Sirmontane still counted.

That was why it had been too easy. Because they'd known that Marco wouldn't leave his men, that of course he'd come to rescue them. That every single one of his team mattered to

Marco; he wouldn't leave any of them behind to be tortured and hurt.

So, by coming to the rescue, by doing the predictable thing, Marco had put them all in danger. He cursed mentally. What an idiot. And he'd thought he'd been so clever, devising the rescue plan.

The first Jeep hadn't stood a chance. It had driven right over the bomb, setting it off. The pieces would be scattered everywhere, along with the remains of its occupants. There hadn't even been the usual warnings of large rocks or whatever blocking the narrow road; at least in those circumstances they knew that any possible alternative route was likely to be rigged and could check it out. The insurgents had been one step ahead, meaning that Marco's team had driven straight over a buried explosive device.

'Pedro? We need to get out. Now.'

'Uh…' came the response.

Concussion, probably. But Marco didn't have time to be sympathetic. 'We have to take cover,' he said urgently. 'Look, I'll come and get you out.' He raised his voice. 'Everyone in the back, be prepared to evacuate and take cover.'

His hand hurt. It felt like a thousand needles burning into his skin. But he'd deal with that later. First of all, he needed to get his men to safety. What was left of them.

It took an effort to shoulder the door open, but he did it. He went round to the other side of the Jeep to pull the passenger door open and help Pedro out when he realised that something was wrong. He couldn't bend the fingers on his left hand.

Which meant it was useless; he couldn't even hold a gun, much less fire one, in this state.

Blood was oozing out of his hand, leaving a trail that just about anyone could follow. He swore, ripped a bit off his shirt and wrapped it round his hand to stanch the bleeding, and used his other hand to yank the door open.

Pedro was still groaning, but Marco was able to get him out of the Jeep, then move to the back and help the rest of his men out. Once he'd got them hidden in nearby vegetation, he used his elbows to propel himself to a better vantage position. Hopefully they'd been near enough to the camp for the blast to have been spotted on surveillance equipment, and help would arrive before things got really sticky.

He could see insurgents swarming all over the Jeep, and Marco prayed to the God he'd stopped believing in that something would happen before they searched the area and found his team.

Amazingly, his prayers were answered: screeching tyres and rapid bursts of fire drove the insurgents off.

'Thank you,' he whispered.

He could hear people calling. Knowing it was safe to do so, he yelled back. Got their attention. Help was on its way.

And finally the pain in his hand made him pass out.

CHAPTER ONE

MARCO CAME TO in unfamiliar surroundings, and tried to sit up. An arm held him down. 'Stay there, Capitán.'

'Where am I?' he asked.

'Back at base. In the hospital.'

Marco forced himself to focus. He recognised the medic from times when he'd treated some of Marco's team. 'Dr Herrera. How are my men?'

'We need to talk about you,' Dr Herrera said.

'We need to talk about my men,' Marco corrected. 'Were there any survivors from the first Jeep?'

'No, but all of those from your vehicle are safe. Some of them have impact trauma from the crash, but nothing too serious.'

Marco absorbed the information. 'OK. I need to talk to their families. The dead soldiers'. Tell them what happened. Apologise for not keeping them safe.'

'You need to listen to me,' Dr Herrera said,

'unless you want to lose the use of your hand permanently and be invalided out of the army.'

That got Marco's attention. Stop being a soldier? His mother would be ecstatic, he knew; but in his own view it was unthinkable. This was what he was born to do. 'Give me the bottom line,' he said.

'You have a flexor tendon injury.'

At Marco's blank look, Dr Herrera explained, 'The flexor tendons connect the muscles of your forearm to the bones of your thumb and fingers. They let you bend your fingers, and the extensor tendons let you straighten them again.'

Remembering what had happened when he'd tried to open the door of the Jeep, Marco tried to bend his fingers. His index and middle finger wouldn't move, and his hand hurt like hell.

Dr Herrera rolled his eyes. 'Well, you can see that for yourself. I take it the window came in and you put your hand up to shield your eyes?'

'Yes.'

'Some glass shards must have severed the tendons. They won't heal themselves, because the tension in the tendons causes them to pull apart when they're broken—think of them working like a bicycle brake cable.'

'So I need surgery?'

'Microsurgery. And it needs to happen within twelve hours. Twenty-four at most. The longer it takes, the more likely it will be that scarring develops on the ends of the severed tendons.'

'Which means?' Marco prompted.

'Bottom line: you'll get less movement back in your hand.'

It was enough to convince Marco. 'OK. Do what you have to.'

Dr Herrera shook his head. 'I won't be the one operating. You're going to need specialist plastic surgery as well, once the tendons have been stitched and the wound has healed. We have a twelve-hour window from when it happened to getting you into theatre. Say two hours getting you back here from the site of the bomb, seven hours between here and London and an hour's transfer between the airport and hospital...' He grimaced. 'I need you on a plane to London now.'

Marco frowned. 'My men need me.'

'You wanted the bottom line, yes? Right now you're not much use to them, and you'll be even less use if you don't get your hand fixed,' Dr Herrera pointed out. 'I want you on a plane to London so they can operate.'

Marco's boss, Comandante Molina, came striding in and clearly overheard the last bit. 'You know the rules, Marco. Medical orders outrank military ones.'

Royal ones, too, Marco thought grimly.

'Get on that plane and get fixed up,' Comandante Molina ordered.

'What about my men?' Marco demanded.

'I'll sort out the medical side and fix them up again, good as new,' Dr Herrera promised.

'And I'll talk to the families,' Comandante Molina said.

'You seriously want me to go London?' Marco asked with a grimace.

'To the Hunter Clinic. Leo and Ethan Hunter. They have an excellent reputation for treating injured soldiers. One of them used to be an army doctor,' Comandante Molina said.

The Hunter Clinic. Marco had heard that name before. Marianna—his older brother Ferdinand's fiancée—had visited the clinic earlier this year for a blepharoplasty. And she'd had other work done there, too. 'I thought they just did cosmetic stuff.'

'They specialise in reconstructive surgery as well as cosmetic surgery. Burns, microsurgery.' Comandante Molina folded his arms. 'They have hand specialists. Which is what you need.'

Well, if his boss was insistent on it, it didn't look as if Marco was going to have much choice in the matter. Even so, for the sake of his men, he gave it a try. 'Why can't I be treated here? Surely it's better for everyone's morale if I'm treated here instead of being flown out to London as a special case. I don't want everyone thinking I get treated differently just because of who my parents are.'

'It's nothing to do with that. We can't guarantee to hold the media off. Not now you've been injured,' Comandante Molina said. 'Though I admit that, yes, your mother has views on the subject.'

His mother hated him being a soldier on active duty, worrying constantly that he was in danger and would get hurt. Marco had had enough conversations with her on the subject. And the injury to his hand would make her worries increase exponentially. Giving a little ground now might make it a bit easier on his mother.

'She wants me out of here, doesn't she?'

Comandante Molina said nothing but gave him a sympathetic look.

'OK,' Marco said, resigned. 'I'll go to London. But only for as long as it takes to get me fixed. I intend to be back on duty as soon as possible.'

'Marco, your dedication has never been in doubt,' Comandante Molina said softly. 'And your men know you don't think of yourself as any different to them. If this was Pedro sitting here, not you, wouldn't you be demanding that he gets the right medical treatment in the right place?'

'You have a point,' Marco acknowledged.

'So listen to Herrera, here, and do what he tells you.'

Marco said nothing.

'While you were out cold I flushed your hand with saline to get the grit out and avoid infection setting in. I need to give you a tetanus shot now,' Dr Herrera said. 'Antibiotics are controversial but, given that you're travelling for hours to another country for surgery, I'd rather you had them now to avoid the risk of infection.'

'Fine. Do whatever you need to,' Marco said.

'Thank you.' Dr Herrera smiled at him. 'I've spoken to the surgeon in London. He doesn't want me to suture your skin as your palm is a mess. I'm just going to dress your wound so it holds until you get to London.'

He talked Marco through what he was doing: a petroleum-impregnated gauze for the first layer of the dressing, to stop the wound sticking to it. Then another layer of gauze, this time soaked in saline but with the excess fluid wrung out, to let any blood escape and avoid a haematoma forming. The third layer was gauze fluff for padding, topped by a loose wrap, and finally there was cast padding with a fibreglass splint to protect the wound from further injury.

'There's a helicopter on standby to take you from the airport to the clinic,' Comandante Molina said. 'We'll talk later.'

'Right,' Marco said wryly to his boss's retreating back.

He was pretty sure his mother would put pressure on his father now to make sure his tour of duty was over, and the injury—even though it wasn't life-threatening—would probably make his father agree and put pressure on Comandante Molina to give Marco an honourable discharge. And there was only one circumstance in which Marco would accept that.

'When the tendons are repaired and the wound's healed,' he said to Dr Herrera, 'is the injury going to affect the use of my hand at all? Can I still do my job?' And he knew the doctor would understand what he wasn't asking: would he be able to work alongside his men without putting them in danger because his hand would be too weak for the job?

'I'm not going to lie to you,' the doctor said. 'There may be some loss of movement in your hand. It's your flexor tendon that was severed, which means it's likely to affect the strength of your grip.'

Loss of movement. Loss of grip. His left hand. The hand Marco needed to steady a rifle or change a magazine in a machine gun.

And it also could affect him playing his guitar again; with a classical guitar, you needed a strong grip to press the strings against the neck. Playing the guitar was what always calmed Marco down and swept away the stress.

If he couldn't do the job he loved…well, then he could still do his duty to his family and his country. Marco had always known that one day he'd have to leave his military career behind and go back to his royal duties. But he hated the pressure of that world. And if he was going to lose the one thing that could always soothe his soul, what would his life become?

Eight hours later, Marco was in London, sitting in a waiting room at 200 Harley Street. Everything about the place was discreetly luxurious: polished marble floors, white leather sofas, chandeliers, soft lighting. It felt more like a luxury hotel than a clinic. Though, for all Marco cared, the clinic could have been a shack thrown up out of corrugated iron and bits of reused timber.

He just wanted his hand fixed.

And for life to be back as normal.

Preferably yesterday.

OK, so the surgeon who was meant to be sorting him out had been called to see a patient urgently. Marco could understand that. He knew he wasn't the only patient at the clinic. He probably wasn't from the richest family or the most titled family there, either; the little time he'd had to glean information from the internet had told him just how exclusive this place was.

But the longer he waited, the more use of his hand he'd lose. And he really wasn't prepared to accept that.

'But, Ethan, you're Leo's brother. Surely you should be the one to head the Hunter Clinic in Leo's absence,' Declan said.

Ethan shrugged. 'You're Leo's second in command.'

'But *you* have the Hunter name.'

Yeah. And didn't he know it. The albatross round his neck. 'Declan, you've worked for it. I don't have a problem with you being in charge.'

Ethan was aware that the other surgeon was eyeing him curiously. Probably wondering if he and Leo had had yet another row and this was Ethan's way of getting his own back. It probably had something to do with it. But Ethan knew that Declan would never ask. The Irish doctor was charming, yet he kept people at arm's length and he knew to keep out of other people's sore spots.

'And you're better at PR than I am,' he added.

'That's the Blarney Stone for you,' Declan

said lightly. 'Ethan, are you quite sure about this?'

'It's the right decision for the clinic. And the clinic's what matters, right?'

Declan nodded. 'Then, thanks. I'm happy to do the job.'

'Good.' One problem down. At least for a little while. 'I have a patient to see. Catch you later?' Ethan asked.

'Laters,' Declan said with a smile.

Just as Marco was about to go and find someone and ask—very politely, and through gritted teeth—if they could give him any idea how much longer he'd have to wait, a man walked into the room.

Well, *limped*.

He was about six foot two—Marco's own height—with dark brown short hair, dark brown eyes, and stubble that Marco thought privately was just on the wrong side of what women found sexy. If this was the doctor and he didn't give a damn about his appearance, did it follow that he also didn't give a damn about his job? Or was this guy some kind of porter?

'Ethan Hunter,' the man drawled.

One of the Hunter brothers, then. Surgeon. The one who was going to treat him?

He didn't try to shake Marco's hand. 'Sorry to keep you waiting.'

Marco had the distinct impression that the other man wasn't sorry at all. There was an edge to his tone, though right at that second Marco couldn't work out why.

'And I'm sorry it's me you're seeing rather than my brother—he usually does the royals and celebs, but rather inconveniently he's gone on honeymoon.'

Royals and celebs, hmm? Suddenly it was clear: Ethan Hunter had an issue about that kind of lifestyle. He'd automatically assumed that just because Marco was the younger prince of Sirmontane he was an over-privileged, thoughtless and selfish socialite. And Marco was in just enough pain now not to be able to rise above it. If Hunter wanted attitude, then he'd get it. Every damn step of the way.

'So how did you do it?' Ethan asked.

'How do you think? Skiing, drinking with my celeb friends and guffawing so hard at the peasants I didn't look where I was going, fell over and severed my tendons,' Marco drawled.

Ethan gave him a level stare. 'How about the truth?'

Common sense kicked back in. Hunter needed to know what had happened because it might affect the way he fixed the damage. Dr

Herrera should have briefed him fully, but then again maybe Hunter was the thorough type and didn't just take other people's words for granted. Marco himself never accepted a brief without asking questions to make sure that nothing had been missed. Maybe Hunter was the same.

'I was in a convoy of Jeeps. The one in front of me drove over a bomb. My windscreen imploded and I put my hand up to protect my eyes.' Judging by the mess of his hand, that was just as well—or he'd be blind as well as having a potentially useless hand.

'Bomb.' Ethan stiffened. 'I see.'

Interesting, Marco thought. Was this the brother who'd been an army doctor? Marco shrugged with the shoulder that wasn't strapped up. 'I was in Afghanistan.'

'You were a soldier.'

'*Am* a soldier,' Marco corrected. 'And I hate being cooped up instead of being where I belong, leading my men and sorting out that whole mess out there. Making a difference. Making things better. But…' He blew out a breath. 'I guess it's still no excuse for being rude to you just now.' He'd been unprofessional and let the pain get to him when he should have known better—both from growing up as a prince in the glare of the public eye, and then from his

military training. Time to defuse the situation.
'I apologise.'

'I apologise, too,' Ethan said, surprising him.
'Just because you're rich and royal, it doesn't
mean that you're...' He grimaced.

Marco knew exactly what he meant. It was
something that he hated himself, particularly in
some of the people who liked hanging around
his brother. He gave a mock braying laugh, and
grimaced back. 'Pampered.'

Ethan seemed to relax at last. 'Yeah.'

'You were out there, too?'

Ethan shrugged. 'That's not important.'

'When did you get hit?'

Ethan's eyes narrowed. 'What makes you
think I was hit?'

Marco nodded at his own arm and Ethan's
leg. 'Different limb, same kind of pain.'

They shared a glance, and Marco knew that
Ethan Hunter understood the rest of it. The frustration of being stuck here when your heart was
back there.

'What have they done so far?' Ethan asked.

'Flushed my hand to clean it, put on a dressing. I take it you were the one who said not to
suture my palm?'

'Yes. Can you feel anything in it still?'

'I'm not sure,' Marco admitted. 'The pain's
gone into a blur.'

'Was it just glass, or is there anything else I need to know about?'

'Glass, mainly. Maybe a bit of dirt. But Herrera cleaned me up.'

Ethan nodded. 'Glass isn't going to show up brilliantly in radiography. I need to give you a CT scan to make sure all the glass is out and nothing else is lurking in there, and then I'll do the op.'

The scan seemed to take for ever. But finally Ethan Hunter was satisfied.

'No more glass. Good. OK, what I'm going to do is open up the wound so I can find the cut ends of your tendon, and then I'm going to stitch them back together. I'll put a splint on to protect the repair. Your skin's a mess, so you might need plastics—we'll see what it looks like when your hand's healed. And you'll need physio to get that hand working properly again.'

'Right. So how long will I be in the clinic?'

Ethan looked thoughtful. 'This happened nearly twelve hours ago and you've flown a long way. I want you in here for the next twenty-four hours so I can keep an eye on the repair. Theoretically, then you could go home. But, given who you are and the fact that you'll have the press hounding you all the way between your place and here when you come in for treatment...' He rolled his eyes. 'And we can certainly do without them hanging round outside and getting in the way while they wait for a glimpse of you.'

Marco could do without that, too. 'I don't want the press knowing I'm in England. If the story blows, then I might not be able to resume my tour of duty. It'll put my men at risk.' The ones that were left. The ones that hadn't been killed, thanks to his wrong judgement call.

Ethan nodded. 'Then you're better off staying here for a while. You'll need to see the hand therapist in any case.'

Marco frowned. 'But if I do go home after a few days, can't the hand therapist come to me?'

Ethan gave him a look that said very clearly, *Stop being a spoiled rich prince.* 'You're not her only patient.'

'Of course. Sorry. Patience isn't one of my... um...virtues.'

That earned him half a grin.

'Thank you. For sorting this out.'

Ethan shrugged. 'You don't need to thank me.'

Marco knew why he'd said it. 'Because it's your job,' he said quietly. 'That's what you did out there, too.'

Ethan turned away so Marco couldn't read the expression in his eyes—which in itself told Marco a lot. He'd seen that a few times before, in other people. So he was pretty sure that something had happened out there and Ethan Hunter didn't want to think about it.

'I need to get you in the operating theatre,' Ethan said. 'I'll do the repair under a general anaesthetic because it's fairly complex. It should take about an hour; though it might be longer if I find more damage once I open up your hand.'

'I'd rather not be out cold.'

Ethan rolled his eyes. 'OK, Zorro, if you want to be a hero.'

'Zorro?' Marco narrowed his eyes at him.

Ethan didn't look away or flinch; he clearly wasn't fazed by who Marco was.

'OK,' Marco said, 'I admit I learned to fence at school, and I did some training with the Sirmontane international fencing team.' Not that he was going to boast about the gold medal he'd won. He didn't need to score points with Hunter.

Ethan shrugged. 'I picked the right name for you, then. Probably that's what your men call you when they don't think you can hear them.'

For the first time in what felt like half a lifetime, Marco heard himself laugh. 'Yeah, probably. OK. If you need me out totally, then fine. Do what you have to. But make it quick.'

'Is this your sword arm?' Ethan asked.

'No. It's my fret hand.'

'You play guitar, too?' Ethan feigned a yawn.

'You're such a cliché, Zorro. Do you dance flamenco as well?'

'Flamenco's dull. I prefer tango.' Marco waited a beat. 'You get better sex after a tango.'

Ethan grinned. 'Probably just as well you won't be playing guitar for a while.' Then he sobered. 'Don't flirt with my female staff, Zorro. Any of them.'

'As if I would,' Marco said, enjoying himself now. He had a feeling that he and Ethan Hunter could be friends. Scratchy friends, maybe. But still friends. Because they each understood where the other was coming from.

Another busy day ahead, Becca thought as she walked up the steps to 200 Harley Street. And that was just how she liked it.

Or maybe not, she thought, as she walked into the reception area to find the clinic's Head of PR in a smooch with her new husband.

'Put the surgeon down, Lexi,' she said with a smile.

'Very funny.' Lexi gave Iain a last kiss and waved him off to his consulting room. 'Actually, Becca, you're just the woman I wanted to see.'

'Oh, yes?' Becca asked carefully. Usually this meant that Lexi was planning a PR campaign and wanted to talk the staff into doing something crazy. If Lexi had been anyone else,

Becca would have made a polite murmur and avoided her, but Lexi was one of the few people she'd grown close to. Not quite close enough to confide in her about the past, but she was the nearest Becca had to a friend.

'I wanted to give you the heads-up on our new patient. Well, he's going to be yours. He's in Theatre with Ethan right now.' Lexi shepherded Becca towards her office. 'He's a bit high-profile—'

'So we need to keep everything under wraps.' Becca rolled her eyes. She was familiar with the drill. 'Got it.'

'I know you're the soul of discretion—but I wouldn't be doing my job properly if I didn't dot all the *I*s and cross all the *T*s,' Lexi pointed out gently.

'I know.' Becca smiled at her. 'Sorry. I guess I got out of the wrong side of bed this morning. So tell me about my patient.'

'A prince, no less.'

Becca wasn't that impressed, knowing that the clinic had an A-list clientele. 'What's he in for?'

'Flexor tendon. He was injured on a tour of duty, so that's another reason we want it kept under the media's radar.'

'A soldier prince?' Despite herself, Becca was intrigued.

'Young, tall, dark and handsome,' Lexi intoned. 'Prince Charming.'

A heartbreaker, then. Becca had met the type before. And been stupid enough to get her own heart broken by one, at a time when she'd still been dragging her life back out of the gutter.

Most of the women at the children's aid camp in South Africa had fallen under Seb's spell; but, knowing that men couldn't be trusted not to hurt you, Becca had avoided Seb like the plague. She'd been so determined to stay in the safety of her shell. But Seb had been patient. He'd made her feel special, had spent time talking to her about everything under the sun. And finally she'd relaxed with him and let him bring her out of herself. In the process, she'd fallen deeply in love with him. Enough to give herself to him. She'd even let herself dream of a future with him…

And then he'd left. Without even saying goodbye. He'd abandoned her. And the lesson had been branded on her heart: the only person she could ever really rely on was herself. Which was why she'd kept people at arm's length and dedicated herself to her career ever since.

Lexi frowned. 'Are you all right, Becca?'

Wild horses wouldn't drag the truth from her. 'Sure.' She faked a smile.

Luckily it was convincing enough, because

Lexi continued, 'Even covered in mud, and looking as if he hasn't slept for days, our prince is sex on a stick.'

Becca groaned. 'And here's you married for about five seconds. Shouldn't you still be in the disgustingly loved-up stage, too busy to notice other men?'

'I'm married, not blind.' Lexi grinned. 'And don't tell Iain I said that.'

Becca just laughed. 'Right. I have patients to see. Catch you later.'

After the operation, Marco woke in the recovery room. It was warm and comfortable and he wanted to go back to sleep.

Except then he threw up. Violently.

'OK. We've got you.' Gentle hands wiped his face clean and helped him sit up.

'I'm sorry,' he said to the nurse.

'Don't worry. It happens all the time.'

Right at that moment, Marco was really grateful for her kindness.

'You're round, then?' Ethan asked, coming over to him.

'Uh-huh.' And his mouth felt disgusting. 'Did it work?'

'We'll see.'

'My arm feels numb and floppy.' Which was enough in itself to make him panic. And it was at that point that he noticed it was propped up on pillows. 'Does this mean I can't use it?'

'It's completely normal for your arm to feel numb and floppy after an op. And the pillows are there to support your arm and keep it elevated—that controls any potential swelling. I want your arm up at shoulder level and your hand above your heart, and you need to use pillows to support your hand when you sleep,' Ethan said.

'Got it.' Marco still felt groggy. 'Though you might have to remind me again tomorrow. I'm not sure how much of what you're saying now is going to stay in my head.'

'Sure.' Ethan paused. 'When the anaesthetic wears off, it will be painful. So don't be a martyr, Zorro. Take the painkillers my team offers you.'

Marco had the distinct feeling that Ethan was talking from experience. What had happened to him in Afghanistan? Had he lost someone—a member of his team, or someone he loved? Did he blame himself for it, the way Marco blamed himself for losing some good men? Had he not taken painkillers as a way of punishing himself?

'So when can I use my arm?' Marco asked.

'The short answer is, you can't. If you try to use that hand before your tendons have healed fully, the tendons will split apart. And, apart from the fact that I don't like having to repeat work, a second repair won't be as effective as the first.'

Marco absorbed this. 'How long do the tendons take to heal?'

'A couple of months.'

Marco stared at him in disbelief. 'No way. You're kidding.'

'And that's only for using your hand for *light* activities. You drive a motorbike?'

'Car,' Marco said.

'Good. That'll probably be OK in a couple of months. A motorbike would take a bit longer.'

'Mountain bike?'

Ethan shook his head. 'Sports you can do a month after that. And then maybe you can start to do heavy activities, as long as you haven't had any problems with scar tissue.'

Marco stared at him, horrified. He couldn't possibly be serious? But Ethan wasn't smiling. 'So basically you're saying I take at least three months off and be a pen-pusher?' Do a safe job while his men faced all the danger. Be a spoiled prince, leading safely from well behind the lines. That *so* wasn't who he was. He sighed. 'That really doesn't sit well with me.'

'Tough. It takes as long as it takes.' Ethan shrugged. 'Don't get that splint wet. You'll need to bag it completely and tape the bag to your arm if you want a shower or bath. Swimming's definitely out—and you don't take that splint off until I tell you or your physiotherapist tells you. Which is probably a month from now, minimum.'

The more Marco heard, the less he liked. 'No exercise. That's not good. I'm going to lose muscle mass.' And fitness. Which would delay his return to the army even longer.

'No push-ups, no pull-ups, no burpees, no weight training,' Ethan said.

Oh, great. That was pretty much his workout routine out of the window. And it definitely confirmed that Ethan Hunter had trained in the army.

'Running? Any form of cardio?' he asked, trying not to let the desperation show in his voice.

Ethan shook his head. 'You need to use your arm muscles to hold your arm across your chest with your hand to the opposite shoulder. So you'll be off balance for running or using an elliptical.' He shrugged. 'No fencing, either, Zorro.'

Because with one arm strapped up he wouldn't be able to balance himself properly. 'So that's a no.' Marco rolled his eyes. 'I'm going to go insane.'

'Very probably, Zorro,' Ethan agreed. 'No horse-riding, no guitar-playing, no...'

'No sex?'

Ethan grinned. 'Not if you insist on being on top, no.'

'I think I hate you,' Marco said.

'No, you don't. I fixed your hand. And I'm good at my job.'

'You'd better be, Clavo,' Marco said through gritted teeth.

Ethan raised an eyebrow. 'Clavo?'

'It's Spanish for Spike.' Marco gestured with his free hand. 'Face. Attitude. The thing you use to cut people open.'

'Technically, that would be a lancet.'

Marco shrugged. 'Clavo will do. You're sure my hand's fixed?'

'Yes. Unless you do something stupid, like try to use your hand too early.'

Marco groaned. 'You're telling me that I'm going to be stuck here for a whole *month*?'

'I didn't say that. I said you'll wear the splint for a month. You'll have physio every single day. Several sessions. I want to make sure there aren't any contractures to your palm, so you need to do stretches and gentle work. You do what the hand therapist says, when she says it, and nothing else. Got it?'

'Because, if I don't, then my hand's gone for good.'

'That's about it.'

So he had no choice. 'OK. I'll do what you say. And the hand therapist,' he added with a grimace.

'Good. Think yourself lucky it wasn't a severed thumb, Zorro. I would've had to replace it maybe with your big toe, and stick leeches all over you.'

Marco gave Ethan a reluctant smile. 'Remind me, which century is this again?'

Ethan laughed. 'I'll have you know leech saliva is the best anticoagulant ever—it's a hundred times more effective than heparin.'

'So I've got nothing to do except pace this room?' And, for the umpteenth time, wish to hell he'd out-thought the enemy. Wish his men hadn't died. Wish he'd managed to get them *all* to safety.

'Like a caged tiger,' Ethan agreed. He paused. 'There's a gym in the basement. It's really for the staff, but patients can use it.'

'I thought you just said I couldn't run or do weights?'

'You can't. The treadmill and elliptical are both out of bounds, ditto all the free weights and the machines.'

'Right.' Everything he was most likely to use. 'Which leaves me what, precisely?'

'The static bike,' Ethan said. 'And *don't* use your arms.'

That was Marco's idea of tedious. A proper bike in the mountains, yes, with steep inclines and rough terrain to challenge him; a static bike, even if it had programmes to change the resistance, wouldn't challenge him at all. 'Great,' he said, curling his lip.

'You can do walking lunges,' Ethan said. 'But that's bodyweight only. Just to be clear, that means not having a bar across your traps, and no using dumb bells, even with your good hand. Got it?'

'Got it.' Marco rolled his eyes again. 'Marvellous.'

'And you can do squats—again, bodyweight only, with a stability ball against your back.'

'What? Like a total novice?' Marco asked in disgust.

'No, like someone who's going to have one arm strapped up so his balance is going to be out and he's not going to be stupid enough to risk damaging his tendons again before they heal. You cross your other arm across your chest like this—' Ethan demonstrated '—and at least this way you can keep your core strong.'

Which was something, Marco supposed. Bodyweight exercises. 'Floorwork?' he asked.

'No. But you can do sit-ups on the stability ball.'

Marco couldn't bring himself to say anything.

'It's better than nothing at all,' Ethan said, and there was a brief flare of sympathy in his eyes.

'I guess.' But Marco was pretty sure that this next month was going to be the longest of his life.

Becca pulled herself out of the pool and squeezed the water from her shoulder-length hair before padding through to the showers. One of the things she loved about working at the Hunter Clinic was the pool in the basement; a swim after work always got the knots out of her muscles and her head in the right place before she headed for her stint at the rehab clinic.

On her way out of the building, she glanced through the glass doors of the gym. There was a man doing lunge walks down the length of the gym; his back was to her, but given the evidence she could see of a strapped-up arm he was clearly one of the patients.

Dark hair, tall, just like Seb...

Her heart skipped a beat.

Stupid.

It had been years since she'd last seen Seb. *Years*. It was about time she put him out of her head and stopped thinking about him every time she saw a tall, dark-haired man. Particularly as he'd made it very clear that he hadn't returned her feelings. He'd left the children's aid camp in South Africa without so much as a word to her. *Dump and run.*

'Get over it, Becca,' she told herself sharply. 'You've got a new life now. And you don't need a man to make it complete.' Besides, she had work to do. Somewhere she was needed.

Shaking herself, she walked up the stairs to the reception area and out into Harley Street.

Over the next couple of days, Marco was thoroughly bored. He tried to be charming to the nurses who came to check on him, but he hated all of this. Being fussed over. Smothered. Suffocated.

Even the gym wasn't a respite. Yes, it meant he could still work out. Of sorts. But he would have been much happier using the top-of-the-range free weights available, lifting until he'd reached his maximum one rep and then pushing himself just that little bit more. Doing a novice type programme just wasn't satisfying. The only reason he'd been able to keep himself in check was the fear of rupturing the repair work on his tendons and being permanently without the use of his left hand. Three months would be tough enough. For the rest of his life would be unbearable.

'You hate this, don't you, Zorro?' Ethan asked when he dropped in to see Marco at the end of the day.

'Sitting here, being useless, when I know I'm needed elsewhere?' Marco scowled. 'Wouldn't you?'

'It's not the easiest thing to deal with,' Ethan agreed. 'You just have to learn to be patient.'

'Is that what you did, Clavo?' Marco asked.

'Just do as I say,' was the level response.

'So you didn't.'

Ethan shrugged. 'This isn't about me; it's about you.'

'I hate this,' Marco admitted. 'I'm used to doing things. Not just sitting here. And your gym is pure torture. All the things I want to use and can't.'

'Patience,' Ethan counselled.

Marco just scowled at him.

'Let's have a look at your hand.' Ethan inspected it, then smiled. 'Good news, Zorro. You get to meet your physio tomorrow morning.'

'So I can start exercising my hand?'

'You do,' Ethan said, 'everything she tells you. And no more than that.'

'Or I'm risking permanent damage. Yeah, yeah. You've already told me.' Marco took a deep breath. Damn. He was being rude again, and the doctor meant well. 'Sorry.'

'Frustration. It gets all of us at some point. Don't worry about it. See you tomorrow, Zorro.'

'*Hasta luego*, Clavo.' Marco sketched a salute with his right hand, and both men laughed wryly.

Becca was still thinking about what Lexi had told her about her new patient. Prince Charming. *Ha*. She'd met men like him before. The last time she'd made the mistake of falling for charm she'd learned the lesson well. In a way, she supposed that Seb had done her a favour. He'd left her at a crossroads. One way had led back to addiction, trying to wash away the pain with vodka—making her mother's mistakes all over again. The other way led to working hard and making the best future she could—for herself, because Becca knew that she was the only one she could really rely on.

She'd made the right choice, and she wasn't going back.

Ethan had said that the Prince was bored. So no doubt he'd be super-charming to her, wanting a distraction from his situation. Fine. He could be as charming as he liked. She'd be sweet and charming back, for the sake of the clinic. But she'd also make very sure that there was a professional distance between them, because she had no intention of being the Prince's personal distraction.

The next morning couldn't come fast enough for Marco's liking. Even though he knew that 'morning' could mean technically anything from one second after midnight until one second to noon.

At last Ethan strolled in to Marco's room followed by a woman in a white coat.

'Zorro, I've got someone you're dying to meet.' He smiled. 'Becca, I'd like you to meet—'

The woman in the white coat stepped to the side and stared at Marco. 'Seb,' she cut in, her voice a hoarse whisper, and all the colour drained from her face.

CHAPTER TWO

'NO, THIS IS Marco—Prince Marco of Sirmontane,' Ethan said.

Prince? What? The man definitely hadn't been a prince when Becca had known him in South Africa at the children's aid camp. He'd called himself Seb. Nothing more. No surname, no nothing. And she hadn't asked for any more details because she'd had her own secrets to hide and hadn't wanted to trade them.

At least he looked as shocked as she felt. That was one thing.

'Becca. I didn't know you were a hand therapist,' he said.

'I didn't know you were a prince,' she said, a little more tartly than she'd intended. Bad move. She didn't want him to know that it bothered her.

'You know each other?' Ethan asked, looking surprised.

Oh, yes. In the Biblical sense, too. 'You could

say that.' Though it turned out she hadn't really known Seb—Marco—at all.

No wonder he'd left without a word. He was a prince, not an ordinary guy, and obviously he'd just been slumming it at the aid camp—something to do between finishing university and starting whatever it was that princes were supposed to do. Which made her relationship with him worth even less than she'd thought.

And how the press would dine out on that if they knew. A girl from the wrong side of the tracks, a girl who'd been hooked on vodka and E, a girl who'd almost ended up in the gutter... and she'd had a fling with a prince.

'Becca—a quick word?' Ethan said, gesturing to the door of Prince Marco's—she couldn't think of him as just Seb any more—room.

She went outside into the corridor with her boss.

'Clearly there's history here. Would you prefer someone else to treat Prince Marco?' Ethan asked gently.

Yes, she would. She didn't want to treat the boy she'd fallen in love with one dreamy summer. The boy who'd played guitar to her under the stars and sung songs of love in a language she didn't know. But she'd seen the emotion in his face and known exactly what the words meant. The boy who'd made her feel so special—and then left without a single word, letting her dreams crash down round her.

But that was an emotional response. And Becca didn't do emotional any more. She'd promised never to let herself get in a vulnerable state again. Yet, two seconds after seeing Seb for the first time in seven years, she was a mess. In shock that the past had come back to haunt her. Trying to process just how many lies she'd fallen for. Trying to get her head round the fact that Seb—the man she'd thought had been an ordinary boy—had actually been a prince in disguise.

With an effort, she pulled herself back into professional mode. 'I'm the hand specialist. It's my job to treat him.'

'Not if it's going to be a problem for you.'

She liked the fact that her boss was standing up for her. Having someone in her corner felt good; it was something she'd never known, growing up. But it also wasn't fair to lean on Ethan and let him make excuses for her. Seb—Marco—whatever he wanted to call himself—was a patient here. Given that he was royalty, no doubt he was only here because of the reputation of the Hunter Clinic. And Becca wasn't going to let any unprofessional behaviour on her part do anything to tarnish that reputation.

'It's not a problem, Ethan,' she fibbed. 'But thank you.'

'Sure?' he checked.

'Sure.'

'So just how *do* you know each other?' Ethan asked.

'We both worked at a children's aid camp. Years ago. I was still a student. He'd just finished university.' If that was true. For all she knew, that could have been another lie. She flapped a dismissive hand. 'It's not important.'

Ethan's eyes narrowed slightly. 'OK. But if treating him does turn out to be a problem just talk to me and I'll get someone else in to cover his case.'

'Thank you. But it'll be fine,' Becca said. Prince Marco wasn't going to break her heart again.

How could you break something that was already broken?

'I guess I owe you an apology,' Marco said when Becca walked back into the room.

'Why?' Becca asked. For being yet another man who'd used her and broken her heart? As if a European prince could give a damn about how an unimportant girl from an obscure family felt.

He grimaced. 'You know why.'

And of course now she was expected to make

it easy for him. Be gracious about it. Or maybe she'd just act cool and casual, as if their summer fling had been just as unimportant to her as it had obviously been to him. 'There's nothing to apologise for,' she said, hoping that she sounded a lot more dismissive than she felt.

'I didn't tell you who I was, back then.'

'No.' She knew it would be hypocritical of her to be mad at him for that. She'd kept her own past a total secret—from everyone else at the camp as well as him. And nobody here at the Hunter Clinic knew about that part of her life, either.

'But I didn't lie to you completely. My name's Marco Sebastian Enrique Guillermo García.'

'Uh-huh.' Becca tried to maintain a semblance of cool. Though right at that moment she was remembering her first introduction to Seb, the guy who was to lead her team at the aid camp. She'd been nineteen and he'd been twenty-one, just graduated from university—well, unless he'd lied about his age as well. And Seb had been the most gorgeous man she'd ever laid eyes on. Tall, dark and handsome, with soulful eyes and a voice like melted chocolate, just a hint of a Southern Mediterranean accent. All the girls at the camp had been in love with him, and when he'd smiled at Becca she simply hadn't stood a chance. She'd fallen for him almost the second she'd met him.

She'd fought the attraction at first, knowing that men couldn't be trusted to do anything else but hurt you; but Seb had been patient with her. Gentle. He'd talked to her, skilfully drawn her out of her shell. It had amazed her that, despite the fact he could've had his pick of all the girls at the camp, he'd actually chosen *her*.

Fast forward seven years to now. There were shadows beneath those beautiful eyes—a combination of exhaustion and pain over the last few days, she'd guess—but Prince Marco was still the most gorgeous man she'd ever seen. And now he was a man, not a boy. The youthfulness had gone from his face, and he'd filled out from being a tall and slightly skinny youth to having hard, perfect musculature.

And his mouth… It still promised sin. The ultimate temptation. A mouth she could remember giving her almost unbearable pleasure. It would be oh, so easy to let herself act on the old attraction.

Well, she was just going to have to resist that urge, because the likes of him were definitely not for the likes of her. And she wasn't stupid enough to jeopardise her career for one of the few sweet memories of her past. She'd worked way too hard for that.

'My grandfather's called Sebastian,' he continued. 'I was named partly after him. So it made sense to use his name—one of my middle names.'

'What was wrong with calling yourself Marco?'

'It would've made it too easy for the press to make the link,' he said. 'And I didn't want everyone thinking that I was just some bored aristocrat slumming it.'

'Weren't you?' she asked, before she could stop herself.

'No,' he said softly. 'I wanted to make a difference.'

She could almost believe him.

Except… 'You left without a word.'

He sighed. 'I was called back to the Palace. My grandfather was ill. It would've been too complicated to explain.'

'And you couldn't have told me that you'd been called home because of a sick family member? You were *that* paranoid about the connections being made?'

'I didn't say that all my decisions have been the best ones—or the right ones,' he said, and looked wryly at his strapped-up hand. 'Or I wouldn't have this.'

'What happened?' she asked.

'Shrapnel. Well, glass,' he said. 'It severed a tendon.'

Which was pretty much as she'd been briefed. Patient: male, late twenties, royal, soldier, severed flexor tendon, needs physio work to regain mobility and movement in his hand.

The last thing she'd expected was for it to be the man who'd broken her heart to the point that she'd sworn off relationships for good and focused on nothing but her career.

Which was what she should be doing right now. Professional was good: it would put some much-needed distance between them. 'Ethan said the repair was a success. So now it's my job to get your hand mobile and working properly again.'

'Is it going to be a problem, Becca?' he asked. 'Working with me?'

She shrugged. 'You're a patient, Your Royal Highness. This is my job.'

Was it her imagination, or had she seen a flicker of hurt in his eyes just then?

Well, tough. He'd hurt her. Badly. And, besides, she was pretty sure it was his ego that was hurt and nothing else. He might think of himself as Prince Charming, but she had absolutely no intention of playing Cinderella. Or fawning adoringly over him. She'd be cool and calm and professional, and treat him just as she would any other patient. With care and kindness, and just a little bit of necessary detachment.

'You can drop the "Royal Highness" bit,' he said.

'What would you like to be called today?' The snippy question was out before she could stop it.

He sighed. 'I guess I deserve that. Call me Marco. And I hope I can still call you Becca.'

Oh, help. The way he said her name. That slight trace of a Spanish accent, so incredibly sexy. It made her knees buckle.

Resist, she reminded herself. This was a job. He was a patient, and she had to treat him with the utmost professionalism. And he was also a prince. They had no possible chance of a future together, and she wasn't going to wreck her career for just a fling.

'I guess. May I have a look at your hand?' she asked.

He indicated his strapped-up arm with his free hand. 'Help yourself.'

Gently, she removed the strapping and took the hand strap off the splint.

Seven years.

She'd changed. Back then Becca had still been a girl. Nineteen years old, a little shy. Beautiful.

Now she was all woman.

Even with her soft curves hidden beneath a sexless starched white coat, with that glorious auburn hair tamed back in a ponytail and those beautiful green eyes hidden behind wire-rimmed glasses, Becca Anderson was gorgeous.

Worse still, Marco knew what it felt like to kiss her. How her body responded to his when they made love. How her breathing changed just before she climaxed.

Ah, hell.

This was so inappropriate it was untrue.

Becca Anderson was his hand therapist, and Ethan Hunter had told him not to flirt with any of the female staff at the clinic.

Ha.

Flirting wasn't the half of it.

What would Ethan Hunter say if he knew just how far things had gone between Marco and Becca all those years ago?

Marco had to get a grip.

Which was half the problem; right now his left hand didn't have a grip. That was what Becca was going to fix.

And he needed to think of her as a medic. Not as a woman.

In fact, he needed not to think of her at all. Since he'd left her behind in South Africa he hadn't let himself think about her. Well, apart from the day after the doctor had confirmed that his grandfather had come through the heart bypass operation safely and would be just fine. Marco had gone back to the children's aid camp, then. For her.

Except she'd left, two days previously, with no forwarding address.

The one girl who'd seen him for himself instead of as a prince. Who'd made his summer feel full of magic. Who'd made him fall in love with her shy, gentle sweetness.

He'd lost her. And he hadn't been able to track her down, even with the help of a private detective; somehow she'd managed to vanish completely.

And all sorts of things could have happened in the last seven years. He glanced swiftly at her left hand. There was no wedding ring, but that didn't mean that she wasn't committed. She might not wear rings to work, given that she was a hand therapist. She could have a family, now. A child.

Besides, she'd made it very clear how she regarded him now. *'You're a patient, Your Royal Highness. This is my job.'*

So he needed to stop thinking about her, right now, and do what he'd done for the last seven years: keep himself busy at work, and then play just as hard with a string of totally unsuitable women. Not let himself think about the girl he'd left behind.

'You've made a real mess of this,' she said, examining his palm. 'How did it happen?'

'Hunter didn't tell you?'

'Soldier, severed tendon.' She shrugged. 'So I'd guess it happened in action?'

'My windscreen was blown out. I put up my hand to protect my eyes.'

'No wonder you severed a tendon. You're lucky it didn't sever an artery and you bled out on the field. Or it could've severed your whole hand.'

'I know.'

Not that it made him feel any better. He'd been over and over what had happened the last two days and nights. Thinking about what he could have done differently. What he *should* have done differently. But it didn't change what had happened. Or do anything to lessen the guilt. He'd phoned every single wife, every single mother, and apologised for not taking better care of their loved ones while they were under his leadership. They'd all been grateful that he'd phoned, amazed that a prince would bother to share his memories of their husbands and sons. They'd cried. They'd even thanked him.

And it hadn't made a scrap of difference. He

still hated himself for making those mistakes. For not bringing all his men safely home.

'Others weren't so lucky.' He sighed. 'Those who were injured have the best possible care. Those who...' There was a lump in his throat and he couldn't say the rest of it.

'Marco, you were in a war zone. People get injured. They die. You can't blame yourself for that.'

'They were acting under my orders.'

She shrugged. 'I take it other people were injured, or killed, following the orders of someone else?'

'Well—yes,' he admitted.

'And do you blame the officers for those deaths?'

He sighed. 'I guess not.'

'Then don't blame yourself. If it hadn't been your orders, it would've been someone else's. I think you're suffering enough without adding guilt to it. You just did your job, Marco.'

How had she become so wise? he wondered.

To his relief, she changed the subject back to his injury. 'The first few days of physio, you're just going to do some gentle exercises. These will help to prevent your tendons becoming stuck in your scar tissue.'

'Stuck?'

'Then Ethan would have to operate again.

And the outcome might not be so good second time round.'

'Right.' He paused. 'I'm under orders to do what you tell me.'

She raised an eyebrow. 'And a prince takes orders from ordinary people?'

Score one to her. 'The rule is, medical orders outrank military orders.'

'What about royal orders?'

He shrugged. 'As far as I know, royal orders from Sirmontane only work inside my country. And right now I'm in your country, not mine.'

'Touché.' She sighed. 'Sorry. I don't mean to snipe at you.'

'But I lied to you about who I was. I can understand you being angry about that.'

'It's not so much that you didn't tell me who you were, it's the fact that you left without a word.'

'So did you,' he pointed out.

She blinked. 'I did not. You were the one who left, not me.'

'But you left the camp without a forwarding address.'

She frowned. 'How do you know that?'

'Because I came back for you when my grandfather pulled through his operation,' he said.

Her cheeks went pink. 'I didn't know that.

And, anyway, what happened between us was obviously just the equivalent of a holiday fling. It was over *years* ago, and we're both very different people now.'

He caught her gaze and held it. Was it over? The attraction was still there, for him. And the way her pupils grew slightly larger when she looked at him made him think that maybe, just maybe, it was the same for her. 'Are we?' he asked softly.

'Yes.' She looked away. 'I worked hard to get this job. I'm not going to let anything put that in jeopardy. You're in London for a few days— maybe a few weeks, until your tendon is healed enough—and then you'll be back to doing whatever it is princes do.'

He raised an eyebrow. 'Which is?'

'How should I know?'

She sounded ever so slightly flustered.

Interesting.

Was it seeing him again? Had it brought back memories? Did she remember what it felt like to kiss him? Was she, like him, tempted to find out if it was still the same between them?

'And it's none of my business what you do,' she said.

'I was in Afghanistan,' he said softly. 'There's a media blanket in place to keep my regiment safe. They don't report anything about me, so my team isn't targeted. Nobody knows I was hurt out there, and nobody knows I'm here. Well, apart from my team back at the base, my family, and the clinic staff here.'

'And you want to keep it that way.'

He nodded. 'To keep my team safe. I guess the media will find out eventually that I'm here.'

'Not from me or anyone else at the clinic, if that's what you're asking. There is such a thing as patient confidentiality. And we're very strict about that, I can assure you,' she said crisply.

'Thank you.' He took her hand with his good hand, and squeezed it lightly before letting her go again.

Mistake.

Because his body remembered the feel of her skin against his. Intimately. And it reacted instantly.

Oh, hell.

Just as well she wasn't looking at anything other than his busted hand. He took a deep breath, willing his body to calm down. This wasn't what was supposed to happen. He was supposed to be following her instructions, not lusting after her.

'Now, you need to do these exercises every hour,' she said.

All businesslike and bossy. And Marco rather liked this new side of Becca. She was professionally confident, rather than the shy teenager she'd been.

'You need to keep the splint on, but you can take the hand strap off while you're doing the exercises. You start with three reps of this one.'

'Three reps?' He smiled. 'You sound like a gym instructor.'

She frowned. 'Stay out of the gym. Any pressure on this hand while it's healing and you'll be looking at permanent disability.'

'I've already had that talk from Ethan. Though he says I'm allowed in the gym to do sit-ups and squats with a stability ball, provided I keep my body balanced and don't use my left hand.'

'That figures,' she said. 'Bodyweight exercises only.'

'And walking lunges.'

She went pink again. 'So was that you in the gym, the other day?'

She'd recognised him without seeing his face clearly? That was even more interesting. 'I didn't see you there.'

'I wasn't there. Just passing the glass door on my way out of the pool. And I assume Ethan told you to stay out of the pool?'

'And put a bag over my arm when I have a bath or shower so I don't get the splint wet.

Yup.' He looked at her. 'But I could spectate at the pool. Do you swim a lot?'

'It's in my schedule.'

So she wasn't going to let him push her into telling him anything about herself. Interesting.

'It's a cliché, you know,' he said, enjoying himself.

'What is?'

'Having a temper to go with your hair colour.'

'I don't have a temper.'

'Don't you, Becca?' he asked softly. 'Or are you just gentle with your husband and children?'

'My marital status is *my* business,' she said coolly.

Maybe, but at least now he knew what it was. If she'd actually been married she would've told him, to put him in his place. Or she would've turned into a proud *mamá* like his sister Arabella, ready to show off photographs of her children at the least excuse.

'Your first exercise, Your Royal Highness,' she said crisply. 'Use your right hand to curl each finger of your left hand down to the top of your palm.' She demonstrated with her own hand.

He couldn't help flinching as pain lanced through his hand.

'Did that hurt?' She didn't sound like a vengeful harpy. She sounded concerned. Caring. But in a professional capacity.

'A bit,' he admitted.

'Did you feel anything pull?'

'I don't think so.'

'Maybe,' she said, 'I need to massage your hand first, to warm up the muscles.' She frowned. 'I'd better warn you now that it might hurt a bit.'

'If it gets my hand working again and it means I can go back to work, then I don't care if it hurts,' he said. 'Do whatever you need to. I'm in your hands.'

She went very, very pink.

Yeah.

He could feel the heat rising in his body, too.

'Lie back with your palm upwards.' She sounded slightly flustered and she was clearly making an effort to be professional.

OK. He'd behave. Even though what he really wanted to do right now was slide his good hand round the nape of her neck, draw her to him, and spend a very long time kissing her.

She pulled a chair round to the side of the bed. 'Tell me if anything hurts.'

Wild horses wouldn't drag that particular admission from him.

He closed his eyes as she massaged his hand. Yes, it did hurt; but at the same time it made his hand feel better. And he liked the feel of her skin against his. Warm. Gentle, yet firm at the same time. Soft. She was near enough for him to smell the light floral scent she wore. She'd always smelled of flowers in South Africa, he remembered. Roses.

With his eyes closed, and mercifully silent, Marco was a lot easier to deal with.

Maybe she ought to tell Ethan that she couldn't cope with her new patient. But then her boss might think less of her—and she'd worked damn hard for her job here. After South Africa she'd thrown all her energies into her studies, graduating with top marks and quickly gaining promotion at the hospital where she'd worked. She hadn't let any relationship get in her way.

Hadn't had another relationship since Marco, full stop.

Until today, that hadn't mattered. Work here and volunteering at the rehab clinic had been her life, and it was good. But seeing Marco again…it had brought everything back. The sheer passion he'd made her feel. The confidence his love had given her.

And then the bone-deep devastation when he'd abandoned her and she'd realised that he was yet another man who'd let her down.

OK. She could understand it a bit more, now

she knew who he really was. Being in the public eye all the time must be draining and it would be hard to know who to trust, who would sell you out to the press.

But she would have kept his secrets.

Just as she'd kept her own. Nobody at the camp had known that she'd spent time in rehab at the age of sixteen. Nobody here knew about those things, either. The past was the past. OK, so she hadn't learned from her mother's mistakes, either with the drink or with the men she'd chosen. But she'd learned from her own mistakes. Really learned. She had no intention of repeating those mistakes ever again. No drink, no drugs, no men—and definitely no heartbreak.

'Better?' she asked when she'd finished massaging his hand.

'Better,' he agreed.

She took him through the first exercise again. 'Good. Now repeat.'

He was a fast learner; she didn't even have to talk him through it, the last time.

'Is that it?' he asked.

'Three reps,' she said. 'And now you do it again, but this time keep your fingers flexed. Use your muscles as you let go with your other hand.'

Again, he did exactly as she asked, and she didn't need to repeat the instructions.

'Good. Last time now,' she said. 'Touch your palm, just using the muscles of your left hand, and extend your fingers back so your fingernails touch the splint.'

He did as she'd asked him to do.

'OK. Now, is your wrist feeling stiff and awkward to move?' she asked.

'A bit,' he admitted.

'OK. Lift your hand up—' she demonstrated the movement '—and let it gently fall forward. Keep your fingers relaxed. Good.' She gave him an encouraging and strictly professional smile. 'Now, back the other way, still with your fingers relaxed, so the back of your hand moves back towards the splint. Better?'

'Better,' he said.

'Good. Last two—your shoulder and your elbow. Stretch your arm above your head. Down. And again.' She talked him through the shoulder stretch. 'Now, bend and straighten your elbow. And again.'

When he'd done the last repetition of ten, she said, 'And that's it for this session.'

'How often do I need to do this?' he asked.

Too often for her peace of mind, given that she was going to be working with him. 'Hourly,' she said. 'So I'll see you later.' Hopefully her common sense would be back in charge before their next session.

'OK. And, Becca?'

'Yes?' She turned to face him. Mistake. Because he still had that make-you-weak-at-the-knees smile.

'Thanks.'

'You're welcome,' she said, and fled.

When she got home from her session at the rehab centre that night, Becca switched on her laptop and looked up Prince Marco of Sirmontane on the internet.

There were lots of pictures of him with beautiful, eligible woman—glittering socialites and A-list celebs. Models, actresses and singers. On a yacht at Monaco. At the film festival in Cannes. Skiing in Sirmontane. He was photographed with a different woman every time— and Marco didn't even seem to have a particular type. Tall, petite, slender, curvy, blonde, brunette, auburn...

The only requirement Marco seemed to have in his girlfriends was that they had two X chromosomes, she thought wryly.

All the gossip columns referred to him as the 'Playboy Prince' and speculated about who would be the woman to tame him. Unlike his much more serious older brother Ferdinand, who was first in line to the throne; Ferdinand was settled, engaged to Princess Marianna. The gossip columns described the older prince of Sirmontane as the perfect king-to-be.

Was that why Marco had thrown himself into his social life? Because he was only second in line always destined to live in his brother's shadow?

No, she didn't think so. Marco wasn't a spoiled brat or he wouldn't be a serving soldier. Besides, she knew that Ethan Hunter had little time for their A-list celeb clients, and yet she also knew that he dropped in to see Marco several times a day for a chat. Maybe they'd bonded over the fact that they both had a military career. But Ethan definitely wouldn't have bothered spending time with the Prince if Marco was shallow and vain and spoiled.

Prince Marco of Sirmontane was a puzzle.

And one that Becca needed to stay away from. For the sake of her own sanity.

CHAPTER THREE

ETHAN CAME IN to chat to Marco that evening and to check up on his hand. 'It's looking good, so far.' He paused. 'So how are you getting on with Becca, Zorro?'

'She's very good.' Marco raised an eyebrow. 'And bossy.'

Ethan smiled. 'Right, on both counts. That's why we hired her.' His smile faded. 'So how do you know her?'

'I worked at a children's aid camp in South Africa for a couple of months when I finished university, before I joined the army. She was there during the university summer holidays.'

Ethan gave him a narrow look. 'That's what she said.'

Marco shrugged. 'So you could say that we're old friends.'

'Such good friends, Zorro, that you didn't even tell her your real name?'

Marco sighed. 'Trust me, being a prince has

its downsides. Half the time people don't see me; they see the money and the trappings that go with who I am. So I'm never sure whether people want to be friends with me for myself, or for what they think I might be able to do for them.'

Ethan nodded. 'That's the thing about being rich. Having socialites for parents.'

'You, too?' Marco asked.

Ethan gave him a rueful grimace.

'But you have a brother, right, Clavo? The one who's on honeymoon?'

'Yes.' Ethan sounded cagey.

Marco frowned. 'So you're not close.'

For a moment, he thought that he'd pried too hard and the surgeon was going to walk out. But then Ethan sighed. 'We have…issues.'

'That's tough,' Marco said. 'I'd be lost without Ferdy.'

'Your brother?'

Marco nodded. 'A lot of people think I should be jealous because he's first in line to the throne, but being the second son—the baby of the family, I guess, as our sister Bella's in the middle— means I get away with an awful lot more than he ever can. I can choose my own job, within reason. Ferdy's life is mapped out for him and he has no choice at all. He's the one with all the responsibility and the weight on his shoulders.' He lifted his chin. 'But I always have his back. *Always*. I would move the mountains of Sirmontane for him if he asked me. Even if my hand was still strapped up and I could only use one arm.'

'So you don't resent him being the eldest and the one everyone thinks is so wonderful?' Ethan asked, sounding curious.

Marco laughed. 'No. I guess I'm kind of glad it's not me. I wouldn't enjoy being king. It'd be like being boxed in. Obviously I'd do it if I had to, because it'd be my duty and I'd never let my family or my country down, but I'd hate it.' He shrugged. 'And, anyway, Ferdy *is* wonderful. He's one of the good guys, and I know if I was ever in trouble he'd be the first person I'd call.' He smiled. 'Ferdy understood why I needed to be on active service for our country, and he talked our mother round. If she had her way I'd be wrapped in cotton wool and not allowed out of the palace grounds. And Ferdy's the reason she's not here right now, smothering me to keep me safe and driving me nuts.'

'You're safe here,' Ethan pointed out. 'I know you have your bodyguard outside the door, but he also checked out our security system and he's happy with it. And nobody here will talk to the press.'

'I know, and it's appreciated.'

'OK. I'll let you get some rest. Oh, and Zorro…?'

Marco rolled his eyes. 'What?'

'Remember what I said. No flirting with my staff.'

Marco knew he was being warned off Becca.

The problem was the warning was too little, and way too late.

Breezy and light. That was how she had to be with Marco, Becca told herself as she walked to the clinic, the next morning. Brisk and breezy and light. Professional. Nothing in the slightest bit personal.

But it was so much easier said than done.

She'd spent seven years suppressing her feelings for him, seven years burying herself in study and hard work.

Yet that first time she'd seen him again it had been as if nothing had changed. As if she was still that young, naive girl in South Africa who'd fallen in love with a boy whose smile was full of sunshine.

But that wasn't who she was any more and he needed to realise that, too.

She nodded to the bodyguard outside Marco's room who, as usual, simply nodded back, and walked in, ready for the first physio session of the day. *Professional*, she reminded herself.

'Good morning. Did you have a comfortable night?'

'Yes, thank you.'

Marco was equally polite with her. Obviously he'd had time to think about it and be sensible, too. Good. That would make it easier.

'How's your hand this morning?' she asked.

'A little sore,' he admitted.

Which might not be good. The last thing he needed now was an infection in the wound. 'Let me take a look.'

She sat down next to him and willed herself not to be affected by his nearness, to ignore that tangy sandalwood scent he wore, as she took his hand and released the strap on his splint so she could take a look at the wound.

But she then glanced at him and was lost. He was staring at her face almost as if he were try-ing to memorise it.

'Marco,' she said softly. 'Your *hand*.'

'Yes.' But now he was looking at her mouth. As if he remembered what it felt like against his. As if he wanted to kiss her again.

Oh, help.

Because now she wanted to trace the curve of his lower lip with the pad of her thumb. Feel how soft it was, how warm.

She never, ever behaved this unprofessionally with a patient. No matter how good-looking he was.

Then again, nobody had been as close to her as Marco. He was unlike anyone she'd ever met. There had been a time when she'd thought he could see into her soul.

And how stupid she'd been. How naive and pathetic.

With an effort, she pulled herself together. 'It's a little bit red. We need to keep an eye on that. I'll tell Ethan and see if he wants you to have antibiotics.' Gently, she put some aqueous cream on his palm and massaged his hand. 'Is that OK? Sore? Stinging?'

'It's fine. Better now,' he said softly, his voice a husky whisper.

This really wasn't fair. That accent, combined with that sexy, husky voice. It just blew her common sense away.

'I have another patient in fifteen minutes,' she said. 'We need to go through your exercises.'

'So you're not exclusively mine?'

She knew he was talking about the situation from a work point of view. Not personal. She dragged in a breath. 'No.'

'Uh-huh.'

He held her gaze for a moment, and she was pretty sure he knew what kind of effect he had on her. What kind of effect he had on most women, according to the gossip columns.

'You never said you were going to be a physiotherapist, Becca.'

'You never said you were a prince,' she pointed out.

'It was complicated.'

'How?'

He sighed. 'I wanted to be seen for *me* in South Africa. Not for my role. Using another name was the only way I could do that.'

It hadn't occurred to her before but, yes, people *would* see him firstly as a prince and secondly as a man. She could understand that.

Though he'd still hurt her. He'd been careless of her feelings. And that she couldn't forgive quite so easily.

He went through the first of the exercises she'd taught him and she watched the range of movement carefully, checking that the tendons were still working and hadn't stuck in the scar tissue.

'So what kinds of things do you treat?' he asked.

'Apart from people with tendon injuries like yours? All kinds of hand problems.' Talking to him about work made this easier. Gave her space. Stopped her doing something really stupid—like taking his hand and pressing a kiss into his poor, damaged palm. 'The Hunter Clinic does a lot of work with burns; as well as damaging skin, burns can damage nerves and I need to help with that and any post-op rehabilitation. I work with people who have carpal tunnel problems and RSI; not just on the physio side. Sometimes I do a site visit and I can recommend changes to the way a workstation is laid out, or alternative work methods.'

'So you prevent the problem happening in the first place?'

'Where I can, yes. Sometimes it's helping with sports injuries—I treat things such as ligament damage and skiers' thumb. Or maybe my patient has a progressive disease such as arthritis, which means their hands are painful and stiff. I can help them regain some mobility and movement in their hands, and work on pain management. I was thinking about doing an acupuncture course as well, so I can offer more than just a TENS machine or drugs for pain management.'

'Adding to your skills? Good idea.' He paused. 'What made you specialise in hands?'

She shrugged. 'The importance of touch, I guess.'

Wrong phrase—because now she was remembering touching him. Remembering the way he'd touched her, his hands caressing her; his touch had set her on fire.

'Making a difference,' he said.

Becca was hugely relieved that he wasn't able to read her mind. And now he'd given her another safe topic: *his* work. 'Like you—at least, I assume that's why you became a soldier.'

He nodded. 'I don't have the patience to be a medic and make a difference that way, but I'm good with systems—I learned that in South Africa. I can see ways to change infrastructures and make them work better for the people they're meant to help.'

'You were good at teaching, too,' Becca said, remembering. 'You were good with the kids.'

'I like children,' he said simply. 'They're straightforward. No hidden agendas. You know where you are with them.'

That sounded heartfelt. She wouldn't have a clue what kind of pressure a prince would face, apart from having to live in the public eye so every single mistake would be picked up and magnified. But it sounded as if Marco was really weary of having to watch every single move and not knowing who was a friend and who was waiting for him to fail.

'You picked up their languages quickly,' she added, hoping to shift the conversation to something a little less painful for him.

'My parents always got me to learn a few basic phrases in the language of any visitors we had, so I could help make them feel at home,' he said. 'Not that I'm trying to boast, but it means I can greet people, say please and thank you and wish them a nice day in twenty different languages. And, actually, it's good to make that effort. I like seeing people relax and be themselves instead of trying to be something they think is expected of them.'

'Your English is perfect,' she said. 'I know nothing about Sirmontane—is English the official language of your country?'

'No—that's Spanish,' he said. 'Though I was educated in England.'

At one of the top public schools, she'd guess. Eton or Harrow or Marlborough. And then Oxford or Cambridge; the other thing she remembered from South Africa was that Marco was very, very bright. 'So tell me about Sirmontane.'

'It's on the Spanish border,' he said. 'It's a mountainous country—we don't have a coastline.'

'So it's cold?'

'In winter, it can be.' He smiled. 'Tourists come for the skiing in the winter and for the lakes and the walking in the summer. We also have a thriving wine industry—it's hundreds of

years old, from the days when monks used to
let the wine mature in cisterns they'd hollowed
out in the stone. And our dairy products are renowned. We have lots of cattle on mountainous pasture.' He grinned. 'I think our chocolate
is better than Switzerland's, but then I guess I
would say that.'

'Lizzie Hunter, our head nurse, is a total
chocolate addict,' she said. 'Maybe you should
get her to do a taste test. She'd give you an im-
partial opinion.'

'Don't *you* like chocolate?' he asked.

Oh, she did. But the idea of eating chocolate
with Marco, being fed one morsel at a time—
especially if he teased her, made her reach up to
take the piece of chocolate between her lips…

She pulled herself together. 'I'm about to be
late for my next patient. You're doing well. I'll
see you in an hour to go through the whole lot
again.' Swiftly and surely, she refastened the
hand strap of his splint. 'See you later.'

Even as she left she knew how much she
wanted to linger. It was probably just as well
that she had an appointment with Mrs van der
Zee to take her mind off Marco.

'Good morning. How are you today?' she
asked as she ushered Mrs van der Zee into the
treatment room.

'A little sore. But I know my Becca's going to make me feel better because you always do,' Mrs van der Zee said, patting her hand.

Gently, Becca removed the splint and examined the old lady's hand, mentally noting the changes since her last appointment. 'The swelling's definitely gone down, so I think that flare-up's over. Did you find wearing the splint at night helped you to cope better with the pain?'

The old lady nodded. 'Much better. And alternating the heat pack and ice pack helped, too.'

Ice for swelling and heat for comfort. 'I'm glad. Are you happy that we work on making your hands a little more mobile today?'

'Yes, that's fine.'

Becca massaged the old lady's sore hands, warming the muscles. She knew that you weren't supposed to have favourites, and she always gave her patients her best regardless of who they were, but Mrs van der Zee was special. Like the grandmother Becca had never had and always wanted: full of smiles and stories of the past.

'Let's start with your fingers,' she said. She talked the old lady through the exercise, showing her how to hold her hand so the fingers were straight and close together. 'Then I'd like you to bend the top and middle joints, keeping your knuckles straight. That's perfect. Now, slowly unroll them again, and we'll repeat it with the other hand.'

From there, she guided the old lady into making a loose fist while resting her hand, wrist and forearm on the tabletop.

'And now we'll work on your thumb,' she said. 'This first one will help you make the joint more stable.' She showed the old lady how to make her hand into a C-shape, as if she was holding a glass or a hand. 'And now we'll stretch it out.' She guided the old lady's hand into a neutral position. 'Try and touch the base of your little finger with the tip of your thumb.'

Mrs van der Zee tried several times and shook her head. 'It won't go that far, Becca.'

'With practice and time, it will,' Becca said. 'And you've done really well, so don't think you've failed. We know how far you can move your thumb now, and that's a really good baseline. We'll work to increase that range a little bit more every time.' She smiled at Mrs van der Zee. 'Last bit, now—we'll stretch your fingers.' Under Becca's guidance, Mrs van der Zee put her hand back in the starting position. 'Now make your first finger and thumb into an O shape.'

'I can do that,' Mrs van der Zee said with satisfaction.

'And now your middle finger.' Gently, Becca talked her through making the same movement with each finger. 'That's great. You're doing really well.'

'Is that it for today?'

'Nearly. Just the finger walking to go, and we're done. Put your hand flat on the table, palm down. That's perfect. Now, move your thumb away from your hand, keeping it in contact with the table. And now move your first finger towards it.'

Once the old lady had stretched each finger in turn and repeated the moves several times with both hands, Becca was satisfied.

'Lovely. You've worked really hard on that today, Mrs van der Zee. And if you try to go through that routine every morning, after you've massaged your hand, it'll make moving a lot more comfortable for you.'

'Thank you, dear.'

When Mrs van der Zee had left, Becca wrote up her notes, then glanced at her watch. Time to go back to Marco.

'How was your patient?' he asked as she walked into his room.

'That's confidential, I'm afraid,' she said with a smile.

'Of course.' He smiled back at her, then went through the arm and shoulder exercises she'd taught him.

She noticed this time that he winced when he lifted his arm above his head. 'Where does it hurt?' she asked.

'It doesn't hurt, exactly—my shoulder's a little stiff.' He looked resigned. 'I guess it's only to be expected with having a sling and my arm being held up like this.'

'Let me take a look,' Becca said, and gently took his arm out of the sling so she could remove his pyjama top.

The worst thing was it meant she was going to be skin to skin with him. Her fingers tingled where they touched him, and she felt her breathing going shallow.

Stop this, she told herself. *Think of him as just another patient. Be professional.*

But that tingle of desire wouldn't go away.

It was years since she'd last seen his naked, muscular back. Sculptors would fall over themselves to use him as a model.

And he was her patient.

Focus, Becca, she told herself sharply. *This is work.*

'Yes, your muscles do feel a bit tight. I'll loosen that up for you.'

Aqueous cream was the most unsexy stuff in

the world. Plain, unscented, and easily absorbed by the skin. Not like oils, which would leave a sheen on the skin and then release a scent as it was warmed by body heat.

This was supposed to be a medical treatment.

She shouldn't be enjoying this anywhere near as much as she was.

And Marco was enjoying it, too. His breathing had changed; it was shallow, almost rasping. It had nothing to do with any kind of medical condition and everything to do with the connection between them, the burning need that sizzled as their skin touched.

He turned round and they looked at each other. His pupils were huge, and she was pretty sure that hers were the same. And that slash of colour across his cheekbones was echoed on hers.

Her mouth went dry, and she really couldn't help sliding the tip of her tongue between her lips to moisten them.

Marco leaned forward, slid his right hand to cup the nape of her neck, and brushed his mouth against hers. The kiss was light, gentle, dreamy—as if they were thousands of miles away from London, under a wide starry sky. Just as it had always been between them. And it felt as if fireworks were going off in her head.

'Becca,' he whispered when he broke the kiss.

She pulled away. 'Marco, we can't do this. You're my patient.'

He shrugged. 'I don't care.'

'I do,' she protested. 'I could get struck off for unprofessional conduct!'

'I'm not going to let that happen.'

Her lip curled. 'Right, and just because you're a prince you can order a professional body to believe that I haven't done anything against the rules? I don't think so.'

'We have unfinished business, Becca, and you know it.'

'I'm your hand therapist. You're my patient. You're in pain and you're vulnerable.'

'Yes, to the first, second and third. Absolutely not to the last,' he said crisply. 'My left hand might not be working right now, but the rest of me is in full working order, I can assure you. I know what I'm doing, Becca. And I want you. I want to kiss you. Touch you. Make you feel the way I'm feeling right now.'

She dragged in a breath. *Oh, help.* She wanted him, too. Just as much.

But.

It was mad. A quick path to getting hurt again. How stupid of her to think that he wouldn't be able to break her heart a second time. Of course he could.

And would, if she didn't stop this right now.

They didn't have a future. Couldn't have a future. He was a prince, and someone with her kind of past was totally unsuitable for him. The only thing he could offer her was a fling. Was that enough? Right now, she didn't think so.

She lifted her chin. 'I'm not going to be like the women you spend your time with.'

He frowned. 'What women?'

'I looked you up in the gossip columns,' she said.

He rolled his eyes. 'They're called gossip columns for a reason—the hacks write what they think their readers want to hear, and that can be a million miles away from the truth.'

'There were plenty of pictures of you escorting different women,' she pointed out.

'Which doesn't mean I slept with them or even kissed them.'

'Who you sleep with,' she said coolly, 'is absolutely none of my business.'

'Becca.' He drew her hand up to his lips and pressed a kiss into her palm, his mouth warm and soft and so sweet that it made her want to cry.

'We can't do this,' she said. 'This is a seriously bad idea.'

'It's the best one I've had in a long time. I haven't been able to get you out of my head since I saw you again.' He held her gaze. 'And it took me a long time to get you out of my head after South Africa.'

He'd thought of her after South Africa? He'd missed her?

Really?

The thought made her head spin. And it would be oh, so easy to give in to the demands yammering through her body.

Marco had been her first lover. And her last.

And she still wanted him.

But if she gave in to the hot tide of desire—what then?

Marco had nothing to lose. He was a prince. Sure, the press might write a few stories about him, but at the end of the day he could do whatever he wanted.

Whereas Becca had everything to lose. Her career. The life she'd built so carefully for herself. Without those what did she have? With nothing left, would she fall back into her old ways? Would the oblivion that a bottle of vodka could bring—and had brought in the past—be all she had in the future?

She couldn't afford to take that risk.

'No,' she said, loosening her hand from his and taking a step backwards in the hope that putting physical distance between them would bring her common sense back. 'You're a prince,

I'm a physiotherapist at the best private clinic in London, and our lives are on totally different paths.' She lifted her chin. 'And if that's not enough for you, I might point out that you've already dumped me once. I don't repeat my mistakes.'

'I'm sorry I hurt you.'

He sounded sincere enough, but she didn't fully trust his words.

'I'm older now. Wiser.'

'But you still can't offer me a future.'

'Is that what you want?' he asked.

It was something she hadn't allowed herself to think about; instead she'd concentrated on her career, working her way upwards and filling her life with work. 'I don't know,' she said. 'Maybe.'

'One thing I learned as a soldier,' he said softly, 'was to take happiness with both hands. Live in the present, don't worry about the future or the past. Enjoy the warmth of the sunshine, the coolness of the rain. Just *be*.'

Where was he going with this?

'Maybe that's what we need to do right now,' he said. 'Forget the past. Don't worry about the future. Just enjoy the here and now.'

If this was the way he talked women into bed,

no wonder the gossip columns were full of pictures of him dating.

'Excuse me. I have another appointment now,' she said, and fled to the safety of her office.

CHAPTER FOUR

BECCA WENT OUT at lunchtime, hoping that a walk would clear her head. It was actually sunny for once, and it might turn out to be the only nice day London had for the whole of June, so she wanted to make the most of it. Only she couldn't just enjoy her favourite summer lunchtime treat of heading over to Regent's Park and walking among the roses. All she could think of was Marco.

She had to face it: she was still attracted to him. He'd made it clear that he was still attracted to her. But it was pointless starting something that could never have a future. Why set herself up for the misery of having to give him up to his royal duty, once his treatment was over?

Besides, if he knew the truth about her, he'd run a mile. Her past could blow up in their faces and cause untold amounts of damage to both of them. The press would have a field day—

and she hated to think what kind of headlines they'd think up.

The Prince and the Addict.

Prince Charming and Vodka-Ella—and maybe they'd put the E in a different colour, just to make the point.

It would embarrass his family, it would embarrass the clinic, and...just *no.*

Yet Marco's words stuck in her head.

Take happiness with both hands. Live in the present—don't worry about the future or the past. Enjoy the warmth of the sunshine, the coolness of the rain. Just be.

Could it really be that easy?

Could they have a fling and walk away intact at the end? If they went into it knowing that it would have a definite end would it mean that neither of them would get hurt this time around?

The thoughts spun through her head, making her dizzy. She had no answers. No idea at all about what to do.

Part of her was tempted to discuss it with Lexi.

Then again, that would mean telling Lexi about all of her past. Not just the fact that she'd fallen in love with Marco before and he'd abandoned her, but the really hard stuff. The way she'd been brought up. The way she'd longed for love but had it taken from her time and time and time again. The way she'd fallen into that vicious circle of needing more and more vodka—and almost been dragged under by Barney.

She couldn't do it.

So it was better to try to keep her distance from Marco.

Marco didn't raise the subject when she called in to run through his physio exercises with him. Part of Becca was relieved; part was worried. Was she just a whim—something to amuse a bored, spoiled prince? Or was she being unfair to him?

She couldn't think straight when he was around, and it made her tetchy. She wasn't used to her world being turned upside down like this. She'd worked hard to keep everything on an even keel, and now everything seemed in jeopardy. The life she'd made for herself, her peace of mind and the walls she'd built round the ruins of her heart.

But on her last visit of the day he took her hand. 'Becca. When are you off duty?'

'You're my last patient,' she said. 'I just need to update my notes.'

'Uh-huh.' His eyes were unreadable. 'What are you doing this evening?'

Well, that was progress. He finally seemed to realise that she did have a life outside the clinic and that she might actually have plans that didn't involve him. Even if it wasn't really that much of a life, if the truth be told: her usual routine was work, a swim, and her voluntary work at the rehab centre, with the occasional team night out to make a change.

For the last year or so it had been enough for her.

Until Marco had walked back into her life.

And now she realised that she'd just been existing, not living.

'I have to be somewhere this evening—it's an arrangement I can't break,' she said.

'Boyfriend?'

She glowered at him. 'Do you honestly think I would've let you kiss me this morning if I'd been involved with someone else? Thank you very much. Why don't you just call me a faithless cheat and be done with it?'

Marco fanned himself. 'Wow. You are woman, hear you roar. I think you're more effective than a flame-thrower.'

Flame? Was this a veiled remark about her hair being red? She scowled. 'Don't make stupid clichéd comments about my hair, either.'

It upset her that she was letting him get to her like this. So much for keeping her cool. If she carried on like this, Marco would guess in seconds that she still had feelings for him. Feelings that she'd thought she'd buried but had still been smouldering without her permission. And now he was fanning the fires again just by being here.

'I'm sorry.'

His apology took the wind out of her sails. 'I'm sorry, too. I didn't mean to snap at you. It's just that I don't do this sort of thing.'

'Just so you know,' he said, 'neither do I. The press is very good at twisting circumstances.' He paused. 'I appreciate that you have other commitments, and I don't expect you to rearrange your life just to suit me, but do you have time to have dinner with me this evening?'

Even if she skipped her swim, she really didn't have time tonight. 'Sorry. Another evening, maybe?' When she could work out how to carve out some time in the evenings without breaking promises to the girl she'd been supporting at the rehab centre. Short of cloning herself.

'How about a cup of coffee, then?' he asked.

'I'm not playing hard to get, Marco,' she said softly.

'But you have a life outside here.' He sighed. 'And I'm being selfish. I should be grateful I still have one working hand and the use of both my legs. Other people haven't been so lucky.' His face twisted. 'Thanks to me, some of my team won't see their kids grow up.'

'You can't change the past,' she said, 'so why beat yourself up about it?' Though at the same time she was wryly aware of what a hypocrite she was; she was just as hard on herself for making mistakes.

'If I didn't care,' he said, 'I'd be less of a soldier. I'd be a monster.'

'There's a difference between caring and wallowing,' she said, 'and you're in danger of wallowing.'

He winced. 'You don't pull your punches, do you?'

She shrugged. 'You need something to occupy your head and stop you brooding about the might-have-beens.'

'A distraction.' He looked straight at her. 'You could distract me.'

She knew that. Just as he could distract her. 'I'm not offering.' Though she could feel her cheeks turning pink. It would be so easy to offer him comfort. And then, once he'd gone, he'd leave her bereft. She wasn't up for that.

'So what do you suggest?'

'I know it's difficult for you, not being able to do things the way you normally do.'

'It's making me a bit twitchy,' he said, and grimaced. 'When I'm stressed, I usually play my guitar. It's got me through any difficult times for years.'

She remembered him playing guitar at the children's aid camp. Songs that everyone knew and could sing along with, so he'd managed to take everyone's minds off things for a while. Pretty classical pieces that had taken her breath away. And then there had been the songs he'd sung privately to her.

'And right now I can't play. I can't use my left hand at all for at least the next month. I *hate* not being able to play. Or being able to do a proper workout in the gym. Or being able to do practically anything else I normally do to relax. As for not being able to do my job... Don't even go there.' He scowled. 'I really hate being so *useless*. Right now I feel like a waste of space.'

'I would offer you a massage to take the knots of tension out of your muscles,' she said, 'but, given what happened this morning, that might not be such a good idea.'

'Yes.' He dragged in a breath. 'I might have to kiss you again.'

The worst thing was, she knew she'd respond if he did. Slide her fingers along the back of his neck. Stroke his face. Tease his lower lip with her teeth, her tongue...

She shook herself.

'Look, I know it's tough—but you have to give yourself time to heal. It'll happen.' She paused. 'Just not as quickly as you'd want it to. And unfortunately you can't change biology. Nothing and nobody can make you heal any faster.'

'I know. I have to learn to be patient.' He rolled his eyes. 'Sadly, patience isn't one of my virtues.'

She wasn't so sure. He'd been patient with the children in South Africa. And with her. Maybe it was just himself he couldn't be patient with.

'I'll see you tomorrow,' she said. And she'd have a quiet word with Ethan on the way out. Maybe he could think of something to help their patient.

Their patient. Marco had a professional relationship with her now, not a personal one. And she needed to keep that uppermost in her mind, rather than letting herself think of him as a man.

By the time Becca walked back into his room for his first physio session the next morning, Marco was a mass of seething frustration. He'd had a whole night to think about it. A whole night to remember what it had felt like, losing himself in Becca. A whole night to wonder what it would be like between them now they were older and had more life experience. He'd never found that particular sweetness when making love with anyone else. Now they were older, would it have changed? Would it still be as sweet? Or was he chasing some distant dream that could never be recovered?

He'd driven himself half crazy with wondering.

Even verbal fencing with Ethan at the end of the evening hadn't taken the edge off Marco's need for Becca. And he'd only just managed to convince the surgeon that it was the frustration of not being able to use his hand that was making him so edgy, not sexual frustration. The last thing Marco needed was for Ethan Hunter to pull rank and decree that someone else would have to treat the prince.

Marco wanted Becca.

In every single way.

And he wanted her *right now*.

'Good morning,' she said chirpily.

'Yeah.' He knew how grumpy and out of sorts he sounded, but he couldn't help it.

She raised an eyebrow. 'What's the matter, Zorro?'

'Don't *you* start with that ridiculous nickname. I get enough of that from Hunter.' He scowled at her.

'Oh, come on. The Spanish nobleman who's a freedom fighter and a dab hand with a sword?' she teased. 'Ethan's right. It's you to a T. You know, I was thinking about getting you a domino mask. I think you'd look cute in it.'

'Yeah, yeah.' He flapped his right hand dismissively.

She sat on the edge of his bed, next to the comfortable armchair he was occupying. 'OK. Tell me now. What hurts?'

His heart.

Which was even more shocking, because he'd never actually let someone get that close to him before. 'Nothing.'

She unhooked the hand strap and examined his palm. 'It's not so red today. That's good. OK. Now lift your arm up.'

'Why?'

'So I can see if there's any stiffness in your shoulder.' She gave him a concerned look. 'You're in a hell of a mood, Marco. Has something happened? Something with your team? You've had some kind of bad news from home?'

He hadn't even thought of Sirmontane for the last day. And that made him feel guilty. He'd been totally self-indulgent and selfish. Spoiled. Brattish. 'No.'

She sighed. 'I know you hate being hemmed in and unable to do much. But, as I said to you yesterday, it takes time for your tendons to heal and it's beyond the laws of physics to speed that up. You'll just have to find something else to keep you occupied.'

'Like what? Playing endless games of patience with a pack of cards?'

'Sure. Or maybe a jigsaw puzzle.'

He closed his eyes. 'I know you're trying to be helpful, but really—can you see me doing a jigsaw puzzle?'

'I guess not,' she admitted. 'So what do you suggest?'

He opened his eyes again and looked at her. 'You could kiss me better.'

There was a long, long pause. And then she sighed. 'I've already told you I can't do that. You're my patient. Anything else is against the rules.'

'Rules can be broken,' he pointed out.

'Not these ones.' She bit her lip. 'Please don't make this any harder for me.'

So she found it tough, too? Oddly, that actually made him feel a bit better. A bit less alone in this. And even though it frustrated him that she clearly felt the same attraction as he did but refused to act on it, he could respect that she wanted to keep her professionalism. 'OK. I'm sorry. I'll back off.'

'Thank you.'

She took him through the set of exercises, barely saying a word except to guide him a little more on the physio. Cool and calm and completely impersonal.

She hadn't always been like that. When he'd first met Becca she'd been sweet and shy. For him, she'd been like a breath of fresh air—she'd made him feel as if he could have anything he dreamed about. And he was sure he'd helped her, too; he'd brought her out of her shell.

Oh, hell. He'd thought he could do this. That he could back off and let her be professional and detached. But, actually, he couldn't. He wanted that breath-of-fresh-air feeling back. The warmth. The sweetness.

This was crazy. It had been tough enough to get over her last time. And he knew that all he could offer her was a fling, and that wasn't fair to her. He couldn't offer her anything more because he had a duty to his country and his family, and he knew he'd have to marry the same kind of woman as his brother was marrying. So for now he'd have to keep his dreams and his libido tightly under control.

Having Becca's hands on his skin really wasn't helping.

He needed a distraction.

Like *now*.

'Becca. Talk to me,' he said.

'What about?'

Anything. Everything. He picked the first question that came into his head. 'Is being a physio what you dreamed about doing when you were a child?'

'No.'

'So what did you want to do?'

'I can't remember,' she said with a shrug. 'It was a long time ago. How about you?'

He raised his eyebrows. 'My job was already pretty much decided for me the day I was born. Until Ferdy and Marianna have kids, I'm second in line to the throne of Sirmontane. There wasn't really another option.'

'I guess not.' She looked curious. 'So what was it like, being a prince and growing up in a castle?'

'Honest truth?' he asked.

'Honest truth.' She paused. 'And it counts as medically confidential, just in case you're worrying about that.'

So she'd worked that one out, at least. Marco was shocked by how relieved it made him feel. 'I loved the castle. The suits of armour, the paintings of knights, the pageantry of the guards marching up and down outside.' He sighed. 'I liked sitting on my *abuelo's*—my grandfather's—lap,' he said, 'and hearing about all the tales of old. The warrior kings, the old legends. I pretty much drank them in. I used to spend hours making cardboard shields and swords.'

She looked surprised. 'Wouldn't your parents buy you a toy shield and sword?'

He laughed. 'Of course they would've done, if I'd asked. But a true warrior forges his own sword. And I guess it kept me occupied for a while. They knew if I was colouring in some intricate design on a shield, it would keep me out of mischief.'

'And being a soldier when you grew up was the closest you could get to being a knight or a warrior?'

'While still doing my royal duties. Pretty much,' he said with a smile. 'I've just never been one for sitting still. Ferdy was always fine, curled up with his nose in a book or drawing. He's fantastic at art. Visiting dignitaries were always pleased with him—a child who was seen and not heard.'

She raised an eyebrow. 'I take it you were the opposite?'

'My mother had to spend a lot of time apologising for me,' Marco admitted. 'I was a bit of a nightmare child, always doing things that I shouldn't—climbing trees, sliding down the banisters at the castle, that sort of thing. I was lucky that we had a fabulous nanny who adored us—and who still works for us, though obviously not as a nanny now.' He grimaced. 'But we also had a very stuffy butler, who didn't approve of me at all and was forever telling tales to my father.'

She smiled. 'And then you batted those incredibly long lashes, and looked up with those big brown eyes, and everyone forgave you.'

'I'm not *that* manipulative,' he said dryly.

'I didn't mean that. Just that you—well, you're charming. I'd guess that you were a hit with all the princesses.'

'The ones of my parents' generation, yes. The ones my age, no—up until the age of about ten they were only interested in boring girly things and they didn't appreciate being introduced to my pet frog. They actually called him slimy,' he said in disgust.

Becca laughed. 'And after the age of ten?'

'They wanted to talk about clothes,' he said. 'Tiaras. Shoes. Lipstick. Dull stuff like that. The ones who liked horses weren't so bad, because they didn't mind getting a bit grubby or pretending to chase dragons. But the ones who were introduced to Ferdy as a potential future queen...' He shook his head. 'That's when I was *really* glad to be the second son. Because I'd hate to have to marry someone I couldn't talk to.'

Becca frowned. 'I've met Princess Marianna. She seemed very sweet.'

'She is—she loves Ferdy to bits and she suits

him down to the ground. But she's not the type of woman I could be happy with.'

Becca couldn't resist asking, 'So what type of woman *would* you be happy with?'

'Someone I can talk to. Share ideas with. Share my dreams with. Someone who can think outside the box.' He looked almost dreamy as he added, 'Someone who's a breath of fresh air.'

Becca knew it was a dangerous question—one she shouldn't ask because she was pretty sure she already knew the answer—but she couldn't help herself. 'So, as the second son, can you actually choose your own bride?'

'As the second son,' he said, 'I don't have quite as much pressure to get married and produce an heir.' He grimaced. 'Though I guess I'm still expected to marry the right sort of woman.'

Any last little wisps of the dreams Becca might have secretly had—that *she* was the kind of woman he could talk to and share his dreams with, and that she and Marco could possibly recapture what they'd had in South Africa—vanished completely at his words.

Of course Marco would be expected to marry the right sort of woman.

Which meant royalty. Or, even if he did choose to marry a commoner, someone from an impeccable background who'd been to the right sort of school. Not someone whose mother had forever sought her own Prince Charming and spiralled into drink and despair when he didn't turn up. And definitely not someone who'd repeated her mother's mistakes in thinking that the answer lay at the bottom of a bottle.

'What about you?' he asked.

'What *about* me?'

'You never really told me much about yourself in South Africa. I mean, helping at a children's aid camp—your parents must've been proud of you for doing something that would make a difference. Especially as it meant travelling so far from home in England.'

Her parents had both died by then. There hadn't been anyone to care, or to be proud of her. 'I guess...' she said neutrally, not wanting to tell him about that or see the pity in his face.

'So you're an only child?'

'Mmm,' she said. It was true enough; she was the only child of *her* parents. She had half-siblings she'd loved dearly as babies, but their fathers had always taken them away after the inevitable break-up of their relationship with her mother and cut all ties with both Becca *and* her mother.

And she really didn't want to tell Marco about all of that. She wanted to keep the past where it belonged. Buried. For good. 'I'm sorry. I have another appointment.'

'And it isn't fair of me to make you late.'

'I'll see you later,' she said, and disappeared.

What was she hiding? Marco wondered. He'd noticed that whenever he brought up the subject of her childhood she either changed the subject or vanished. It was clear that she came from a much more modest background than his own. But did she really think he was so much of a snob that he'd hold that against her?

He mixed with people from all sorts of backgrounds as part of his job, and it had never bothered him whether someone had been to the 'right' sort of school or if they spoke with a regional accent instead of being 'posh'. It was how you treated others that counted with Marco, not where you came from.

Maybe he could get her to open up to him tomorrow.

Maybe.

CHAPTER FIVE

ON THE TUESDAY morning Ethan walked into Marco's room with Declan Underwood, the acting head of the clinic, looking grim. 'Well, Zorro, it looks as if someone's ratted you out,' he said. 'The paps are three deep outside, waiting for a glimpse of you. And we can hardly give our clients the discreet service they expect from us when there are hundreds of cameras out there.' He tossed a tabloid newspaper onto Marco's bed.

Marco glanced at the front page. There was a picture of him in uniform, taking up half the page, with the headline: *Wounded hero returns to London.*

He scanned the text swiftly. Just as he'd feared, they'd run a story about him rescuing his men in Afghanistan and how he'd got everyone out of his Jeep even though he couldn't use one hand.

He shook his head. 'I'm not a hero. I just did

my job—I did what anyone else in my position would have done.'

Ethan looked sympathetic, almost as if he'd been there.

'And you know as well as I do it turned out not to be the right thing in any case. They'd rigged the road and men *died* because of me.' Marco scowled at the newspaper.

'Nobody from here broke the story,' Ethan said.

'Of course not. Apart from anything else, there are details here that only someone from the camp would know. Or their families, maybe.' Marco sighed. 'I'm so sorry you've been dragged into this. I imagine this is going to cause you a few problems.'

'It's going to be a bit tricky for some of our clients,' Ethan agreed.

'So how do we get rid of the press?' Marco asked.

'You need to work with them,' Declan said. 'Give them enough to keep them on side without breaching any confidentiality issues.'

Ethan curled his lip. 'They make up what they want. And they'll dig until they find what they want to see.'

That sounded personal, Marco thought. Had the press trashed him in the past? Or maybe someone close to him? 'They do exaggerate,' he agreed.

'But if you work with them it'll lessen the damage. We need to build a relationship with the press,' Declan repeated.

'That's why I brought him here,' Ethan said. 'Declan's a lot better with them than I am. He's good with the blarney. Not to mention the fact that he sweetened them up last time we were papped by sending them tea and biscuits because it was cold.'

'I just want to do my job,' Declan said, 'and getting the press on our side means fewer delays.'

'You could give them a photo opportunity, Zorro,' Ethan said. 'Perhaps a royal wave from the balcony with your good hand—but do make sure they see the strapping for your war wound so they can see the work we've done on you.'

'Not funny, Clavo,' Marco said, narrowing his eyes. 'I don't give a damn what they say about me—but now the press blanket's been breached it means my regiment is in danger.'

'But everyone knows you're in London. There's no point in anyone targeting your regiment as they know they're definitely not going to capture *you*,' Declan said.

'They can capture others and demand me in exchange,' Marco pointed out.

'As *if* your family would ever agree to that,' Ethan said, rolling his eyes. 'Get real, Zorro.'

'I need to go out there and calm the mob down,' Declan said, 'so our staff can actually get into the building. I think we need to tell them that, yes, you are here, Marco, and, yes, you've had an injury to your hand, but that I can't go into further details because of patient confidentiality; you're making a good recovery and we'll update them as and when we can; and you'd like them to continue their good work in being careful about what they report so they don't put your team's safety at risk.'

'That works for me,' Marco said. 'I'll call my father and tell him how we're handling it. You have a PR team here?'

'Lexi's the head of our in-house team,' Declan confirmed.

'My father's PR team will probably want to liaise with her. Oh, and it's warm outside, right?'

'Right,' Ethan said, looking mystified. 'Why?'

'Because it's not the right weather for tea and biscuits. Send the paps ice creams and cold drinks, and I'll pick up the bill.'

'Now, that,' Declan said with a smile, 'is a great idea.'

'I don't think anyone could miss the press pack outside the front door,' Declan said at the emergency staff meeting that morning. 'I've told them, with Marco's permission, that he's here, we've treated him for a hand injury, he's comfortable and he's making a good recovery. I've also told them that I can't give them any more information, because of patient confidentiality. So if any of them ask you for more, just smile and say he's comfortable, and you're sorry but you can't break patient confidentiality, and I'll update them as soon as I can.'

'Got it,' Becca said. But her stomach knotted in panic. If the press couldn't find a story about Marco, would they start digging elsewhere? Supposing they started researching the pasts of the staff at the Hunter Clinic? They'd broken the story about Ethan and Leo's father, years before. And there had been another story, about the rescue Ethan had been involved with in Afghanistan; Becca could still remember Leo's reaction to that. The shock. The hurt.

With a bit of digging, the press could find out about the sordid mess of her past—and that would cause shockwaves through the clinic. It would mean she'd have to resign. What kind of patient would agree to be treated by a former addict, even though she hadn't had a drink or touched any tablet stronger than paracetamol for more than seven years now?

And, worse, if they found Barney and he told

them what he knew… Of course he'd leave his own part out of it, and the press wouldn't care what he'd done to her because they'd have their story. She'd have to leave the job she loved so much. She might even be struck off the professional register for something that had happened when she was still little more than a child. OK, so technically she'd been over the age of consent, but…

This wasn't *fair*.

Worry made her short-tempered. She was short with Marco when she went in to do his physio—even though she knew she was being grossly unfair, because it wasn't his fault that the press was doorstepping him. Though she noticed that he was equally short with her.

The last few days had been a sweet, romantic dream. They'd been cocooned in a bubble, where perhaps they could start to fall in love with each other again and everything would be perfect.

But now it was time to wake up, face reality, and know that it was over.

'I've spoken to my father,' Marco said to Ethan. 'And his media team has come up with a fix. Tell the press you've done such a great job of mending my hand that I can be discharged from the clinic and move out to my family's London apartment. So there'll be no point in the press camping out here any more, because they're not going to get a glimpse of me—I won't be here.'

'Thank you,' Ethan said. 'But we *haven't* actually finished treating you, have we? There's the small matter of physiotherapy. And if you don't keep up with the exercises, then you'll risk losing movement in your hand. As it is, I'm concerned about your grip. I'd advise very strongly that you continue your therapy.'

'So what do you suggest? If I come back here for treatment, you'll still have the press doorstepping you.' Marco paused. 'Unless your staff could visit me? Although, as you've already pointed out to me, I'm not Becca's only patient. I know my family's place isn't that far from here, but she still wouldn't have enough time to come to me, treat me, come back here in time for her next appointment, treat her patient, and then be back with me for my next physio. Not to mention doing all her paperwork. It wouldn't be fair to her.'

'That kind of routine's not doable,' Ethan agreed. 'But I'll talk to her. If she's happy to work with you on a one-to-one basis, and for you to be her only patient for the time being, then I can arrange a stand-in physio for the rest of her caseload.'

And maybe, Marco thought, once they were

outside the clinic Becca's professional distance might dissolve. In the times when she wasn't treating him they could grow closer. Be friends instead of patient and therapist. Maybe they could even become lovers again? He'd get the chance to discover who Becca had become—and maybe they'd sort out this thing between them and find out what the future held.

He damped down the surge of optimism. 'And if she's not happy to do that?'

'Then you get the stand-in,' Ethan said. 'And may I remind you—?'

'No flirting with your staff,' Marco cut in, rolling his eyes. 'I remember.' Strictly speaking, he wasn't flirting with any of the staff at the Hunter Clinic. But at his home...things might be different. Because then different rules would apply.

'Becca—a word?' Ethan said.

'Sure.' Becca followed him into his office. 'What can I do for you?' she asked.

'I thought you should know that our illustrious patient is leaving this afternoon.'

She froze. Marco was *leaving*? But he hadn't said a word to her.

This was South Africa all over again: he was going without even saying goodbye. Just as well she hadn't let him back into her life, or it would be dump-and-run for the second time.

She schooled her expression into neutral. 'Uh-huh.'

'Which means we're not going to be door-stepped by the press any more, and he'll get the high-level security he's going to need now the story's broken.'

'Of course,' Becca said, trying very hard not to let it show how much she minded that Marco hadn't said a word to her about it in their treatment sessions this morning.

'But,' Ethan said, 'he hasn't finished his physio treatment. Which is where you come in.'

'Me?' She frowned. 'But, if he's leaving, it means he won't be treated here any more.'

'No. He'll be treated at the family apartment.'

She still didn't see what that had to do with her. If Marco was going back to Sirmontane, surely there were physiotherapists there?

'In London,' Ethan clarified. 'And I wondered if you could do it.'

She ignored the flare of hope. 'What about my other patients? I've got appointments booked in between his. And, unless this apartment's literally a two-minute walk away, I won't have time to treat anyone else—I'll be spending all my time travelling between his place and here.'

'Marco needs hourly treatments, which

means basically having a personal physio,' Ethan agreed. 'So I can draft someone in to cover the rest of your caseload, if that works for you.'

'He asked for me to treat him?' She really hoped her voice didn't sound as breathless and squeaky to Ethan as it did to herself.

'I didn't give him the chance to ask for you,' Ethan said. 'I wanted to run it by you first. If it doesn't work for you, then I'll tell him he'll have to have a different physio. Royal or not, he can't order you about.' He shrugged. 'But you're good at your job, Becca. You're the obvious first choice, if you're happy to do it.'

Work one-on-one with Marco. No other patients.

It didn't seem real.

She remembered what he'd said. *Seize the day.* Could she be that brave?

'Yes,' she said.

'Ethan told me you'd agreed to treat me at home,' Marco said when Becca called in to go through his next set of exercises. 'Thank you.'

'It was the best solution for everyone,' Becca said, trying to play it cool. 'Sorry I was a bit short with you earlier.'

He shrugged. 'No worries. It always tends to get a bit tense when the press are involved.'

'So…um…do I turn up to your place tomorrow morning at nine? It might be handy to know the address,' Becca pointed out.

He smiled. 'I was rather hoping I could tempt you to come over later this afternoon…say when you've finished work? And maybe stay for dinner?'

'Dinner?' Did he mean just dinner, or would he expect more than that? Her heart rate sped up.

'No pressure,' he said softly. 'I like your company.'

Becca wasn't sure whether to be disappointed that he didn't want to take things further, or relieved that he was letting her off the hook. 'Dinner,' she said again.

He paused. 'If you're not committed elsewhere.'

How could she tell him about her work at the rehab centre? Even if she told a slight fib and said she was volunteering there because they'd helped a close friend, and she wanted to give something back for her friend's sake, he was bright enough to guess that the 'friend' didn't exist—that *she* was the one who'd needed help from the rehab centre to wean herself off vodka and the other stuff Barney had introduced her to.

She really didn't want to tell Marco the truth

about the whole sordid mess. She didn't want him to know just how low she'd sunk. She didn't want him to know how she'd been hooked. Even though the therapist had tried to persuade her that none of it had been Becca's fault—that with her mother's addiction and the kind of people who'd surrounded her Becca hadn't stood a chance—Becca had never quite been able to believe that. She still thought she should have been stronger.

'I need to make a phone call,' she prevaricated.

'OK.'

'So why aren't you leaving the clinic in the middle of the night?'

'Why would I do that?'

She spread her hands. 'We've had patients leave in the middle of the night before to avoid the paparazzi.'

He smiled. 'No, I want the press to *see* I'm leaving. Then they'll stop staking out the clinic and you can all go back to normal.'

'What about your arm? If it gets knocked in the middle of the crowd…'

He shrugged. 'That's what my bodyguard's for. He'll clear the way. So… Tonight…' He gave her an address.

Becca blinked, recognising the name of the road and the very exclusive development of houses. It wasn't that far from the clinic, but it was too far for her to go and see him and then come back to see her other patients between his appointments, even if she took a taxi between his house and 200 Harley Street. 'You live on the edge of Regent's Park?'

'Yes.' He didn't look in the slightest bit fazed by the question. If anything, he acted as if it was perfectly normal to live in the sort of house that cost more than a thousand times the average person's annual salary. Yet again Becca was aware of the massive gulf between their lifestyles.

'Come over after work,' he said. 'I'll tell Security to expect you.'

'Security?' she asked.

'There's a security gate. Visitors need to sign in. Are you walking or coming by car?'

'Marco, normal people don't tend to drive in London. It's way too much hassle and parking's a nightmare. You either take public transport or you walk.'

'I could send Rafa, my driver, and the limo for you,' he offered.

'Limo?' She smiled. How incongruous could you get? 'Marco, I'm a physiotherapist, not a rock star or a famous actress. I'll get a taxi.'

'If you insist.'

'I do.'

'OK. Our place is about five minutes' walk from the gate. Just ring the front doorbell and Maria, our housekeeper, will let you in.'

A housekeeper, a driver... How normal he made it sound to have staff. Whereas she did her own housework and if she'd had a car she would've driven herself.

'Right. Now, let's take this hand strap off and see how much mobility you've gained in your hand since yesterday.'

'Yes, ma'am,' he teased.

Face the press. OK. He could do this.

Marco took a deep breath, pinned on his public smile, and walked through the front door of 200 Harley Street, his bodyguard at his side.

What felt like a thousand flashbulbs went off, followed by a babble of excited speech.

'Prince Marco, where are you going?'

'Why are you leaving the clinic?'

'Are you going back to Afghanistan?'

Marco held up his free hand. 'Guys, one at a time, please. Where am I going? To my family's home in London so I can finish recuperating. Why am I leaving?' He nodded at his left arm. 'Because, as you can see, I'm fixed. Or at least on the mend—it was a flexor tendon injury, so it will take a bit of time to heal. Am I going back? I hope so, but not until I'm fit. Because I can't—and *won't*—put my team at risk.'

More flashbulbs. More babbled questions.

'Hey, Marco, thanks for the ice creams and the cold drinks!' someone called.

He smiled back. 'My pleasure. I thought it might be a bit hot for tea and biscuits.'

There was a ripple of appreciative laughter. No doubt half the paps had also been here for the tea and biscuits episode Ethan had talked about.

'Thanks, guys. I'm going home now. And can I ask that you don't jog my arm, please, on my way to the car? My hand's still a little bit fragile.'

'You're a hero!' someone else called.

Oh, how he wasn't.

'I'm no hero,' he said quietly. 'I just did my job. It's not my place to talk politics, but in my view the real heroes are the ones putting their country back together and trusting they can give their children an education and medical treatment. The ones who are fighting for men and women to be treated equally.'

There were heads nodding in agreement as he spoke.

'Marco, will you have a string of beautiful women to mop your brow while you recuperate?' another one of them called.

Marco laughed. 'I'm afraid that's not actually in my doctor's orders. I just have to rest and exercise my hand as I've been taught.' He smiled at them. 'I'm sure you can all understand that I'm a bit tired right now—I'd really like to go home, and I could kill for a cup of coffee.'

There were sympathetic grins all round.

'My father's PR team will issue regular bulletins to tell you how I'm doing,' he said. 'And please remember that my team's still out there in Afghanistan. You were great at keeping them safe before with the media blanket. I'd really appreciate it if you could keep up the good work and keep them safe while I'm here in London.'

And finally, to Marco's relief, the press pack parted and allowed him and his bodyguard to go down the steps to Rafa, his driver, in the waiting limo.

CHAPTER SIX

REGENT'S PARK WAS a place where you'd go to have a picnic by the lake, or to visit the zoo or the gardens. The place Becca had desperately wanted to visit as a child, after reading *The Hundred and One Dalmatians* and discovering that Pongo the Dalmatian was walked there by Mr and Mrs Dearly. The place she sometimes went to in her lunch break, as they had the biggest collection of roses in London, and Becca had always loved the scent of roses.

It definitely wasn't a place where you actually lived. Not unless you were from a seriously wealthy background. The nearest Becca had ever come even to renting a house there was on a Monopoly board.

She went to the security gate, as Marco had directed; to her relief, the staff there were expecting her. She showed them her identity card from the clinic and her bank card, to prove that she was who she said she was, signed in, then walked round the corner to Marco's family home and stopped dead.

The house was amazing; it was part of a long, sweeping terrace. There were four floors, the walls were cream stucco and punctuated by huge floor-to-ceiling windows, and there were actually columns holding up the portico—real fluted two-storey-height columns, like the ones outside the British Museum, except with leafy bits at the top instead of scrolls. There was a wide wrought-iron balcony running along the entire length of the house on the first floor, and wrought-iron railings at the front of the house. Behind the railings were raised flowerbeds, and as Becca got closer she realised that the steps leading to the house were marble.

Wow.

Really, she felt as if she ought to be going to the servants' entrance rather than the front door. After all, wasn't that kind of what she was as the prince's physiotherapist?

Lifting her chin, she rang the doorbell.

A middle-aged woman that Becca assumed was the housekeeper Marco had told her about answered the door. 'Can I help you?'

'Hello, I'm Becca Anderson, the physio-therapist from the Hunter Clinic. I have an appointment with…' Help, how did you refer to a prince? She couldn't just call him Marco, the way she did to his face. His housekeeper was bound to expect a properly respectful mode of address. 'With His Royal Highness,' she finished miserably.

'Ah, so you're Becca—come in. I'm Maria, the housekeeper. I'll take you through to the Prince.'

Becca was surprised and relieved by the warmth of the greeting. She followed the housekeeper through the large black door into the hallway. There were marble floors that reminded her a bit of the ones at Harley Street, but there the resemblance ended.

She was used to discreet luxury from working at the Hunter Clinic, but Marco's family home was something else. Maria showed her into a room where the floors were polished parquet and there was a huge rug in the centre; it looked like silk and Becca was almost too nervous to stand on it, in case she put a mark on it or pulled a thread or something.

'Have a seat. The Prince will be with you shortly,' Maria said.

Everywhere in the room was incredibly neat and orderly. There was a choice of beautiful cream sofas to sit on, liberally spread with thick cushions and augmented by Louis XV tall-back cream-upholstered armchairs. There were also several occasional tables from the same period that Becca suspected were original pieces rather than reproduction, and several beautiful floral arrangements in crystal vases.

The lights were traditional chandeliers, which reminded her of the stunning Venetian glass she'd fallen in love with on holiday one year—the kind of stuff that had been way, way outside her budget. There was a gilt mirror over the mantelpiece, and the reflection had the kind of softness that told her it had to be very old glass—maybe several hundred years old, and handmade by a craftsman rather than mass-produced in a factory.

The floor-to-ceiling windows had cream damask drapes and a view over Regent's Park that took her breath away. *Imagine growing up here*, she thought. It was only a few physical miles away from the grotty seventh-floor flat where she'd grown up, but it was light years away emotionally. Here, everything was beautiful and light and airy, instead of dank and chipped or fraying.

The mantelpiece was marble and held a number of heavy silver-framed photographs. Becca couldn't resist being nosey and taking a closer look at the family portraits. In pride of place was what looked like a relatively recent photograph of the King of Sirmontane with his queen, two sons and a daughter; Becca could really see the resemblance between Marco and his family. Marco had the same dark eyes and hair as his father and brother and the same smile as his mother and sister. His older brother looked more serious, but there was a kindness in his face that Becca knew was part of Marco's make-up, too.

Another photograph showed Marco's sister in a wedding dress, with a man Becca assumed was her husband, and another showed them both in a garden with two toddlers, clearly theirs.

She could imagine Marco as an uncle. He'd be the first one on the floor with the children, building forts out of bricks and settling them both on his lap to read them a story.

Just for a second she imagined Marco as a father, holding his newborn child with a tender expression in his eyes. And she suppressed the thought ruthlessly. She wasn't ever going to have a family, and she most definitely wasn't going to have a family with Marco.

There was another photograph of an older man with the three children, though in this one they were much younger. She had a feeling that the older man was the grandfather who'd been taken ill while Marco was in South Africa—a feeling that deepened when she saw a picture of Marco as a child with the same man and a puppy, laughing and looking totally carefree. A picture that tugged at her heart.

'Good evening, Becca.'

She spun round, feeling the colour flood into her face at being caught snooping. 'I—er—sorry, I was being nosey.' Why hadn't she just sat down politely and waited for him as she'd been told to do?

'No worries. Help yourself.' He smiled at her. 'That's the family—obviously my parents, my grandfather, my sister Arabella, my brother Ferdinand, Bella and her husband Luiz, the twins, and that was my little dog Pablo. He was my sixth birthday present from my grandfather, and I loved him to bits.'

'Uh-huh.'

Marco here didn't feel like the Marco she knew. In South Africa he definitely hadn't been a prince; he'd been just one of the other volunteers at the children's aid camp, super-handsome and yet kind and thoughtful with a heart of gold. And at the clinic he'd seemed just like any of the other patients. But here? Here, Marco was markedly a prince. Even the way he walked seemed different—seemed regal, somehow.

What on earth was she doing here? This place highlighted just how unsuitable Becca would be as a prince's girlfriend. This was so far out of her own experience, it was untrue. She needed to keep that in mind and protect her heart. As soon as Marco was fit to go back to work, he'd leave—and after that one goodbye she'd never see him again.

'Would you like a guided tour?' he asked.

'Um…sure.' Though it felt almost like having a guided tour of an English country house that had been left to the nation by the family years before—a snapshot of the past. Somewhere you could only dream of living. Not somewhere that people actually lived for real.

'I guess I should start with the front of the house. It was designed by John Nash and built nearly two hundred years ago; it's a listed building,' he intoned.

Well, of course—where else would a royal family live?

'It's my parents' base in London—obviously it's big enough for us all to be here together, including Bella's husband and the twins, plus any guests and staff.'

Becca didn't dare ask how many bedrooms there were. This was way, *way* out of her league.

'So, this is one of the sitting rooms.'

One of? Most people she knew had only one, and sometimes not even that; in her own flat the sitting room did triple duty as her dining room and her study, too.

'This is the dining room.'

He took her through to the next room. Again, the windows were floor to ceiling, the large gilt-framed paintings on the walls all looked like original oil portraits, and the dining table was so huge that it could have seated an entire rugby squad and then some. The wood was beautifully polished and there were some candelabra at either end that might have been gilt but Becca had a nasty feeling that they were actually solid gold. There was another beautiful arrangement of fresh flowers in a crystal bowl in the centre.

'This is the library,' he said, showing her into the next room.

She caught her breath. 'Oh, I love this,' she said, unable to hold the words back. Like the other rooms, it had floor-to-ceiling windows, with bookshelves between them and covering one entire wall. There were comfy sofas in the centre, with reading lamps nearby, a low table with a chessboard, a grand piano, and also a couple of guitars on stands which she guessed belonged to Marco. This was a room that made her feel comfortable—where she could actually feel as if she belonged.

He sat down at the piano and picked out a melody with his right hand. 'It doesn't feel right, playing something without the harmony,' he said, 'but I guess this is better than nothing at all.' He stroked one of the guitars longingly. 'So how long will it be before I can play again?'

'You can't even lift a kettle for another six or seven weeks,' she said. 'I'm sorry, Marco. There isn't a nice way of saying this.'

'Tell me straight. I'm never going to play again?'

'Not *never*,' she said, 'but playing guitar means using a lot of pressure. It counts as heavy activity, so it'll be months rather than weeks or days before you can try, and even then you'll have to take it really easy. Play for a couple of minutes, rather than hours.'

'I guess I have to learn to take things slowly, or I'll do more damage that even Ethan Hunter won't be able to fix it.' He looked utterly miserable.

Hating the fact that he was so unhappy and unable to resist trying to comfort him, Becca walked over and hugged him. She knew this was a bad idea—she ought to keep some professional distance between them—but how could she stand by when he was so dejected?

Marco wrapped his good arm round her and rested his forehead against hers. 'Thank you. I needed that. I just hate being so helpless and having to rely on other people to help me. I'm used to doing things myself.'

'Action hero,' she said softly.

He shook his head. 'I'm no hero, Becca. I just do my job, and I try to do it well.'

She guessed that Marco would be good at just about anything he did. Second best would never be enough for him.

'And this time I messed it up,' he said, confirming what she'd just thought.

He was so hard on himself. Why?

'I could hold the guitar for you,' she suggested. 'If you told me what notes to play, you could still do the strings with your right hand.'

His lips brushed against hers, a feather-light touch. She thought it was probably meant to be a token of gratitude, but all it did was make her tingle all over and want more. To the point where she could feel herself on the cusp of hyperventilating.

'That's such a sweet offer. Do you actually play the guitar, Becca?'

'Um—no,' she admitted. 'I never learned to read music or anything like that, and you're the only person I've ever met who actually plays an instrument.'

'Then I'd probably end up barking orders at you and getting frustrated because I couldn't explain myself well enough to you, and—well, I'd be horrible,' he said. 'And I don't want to be horrible to you. But thank you for offering. I appreciate it.'

He held her just a little bit closer, then released her. She guessed that he was just as confused about this as she was. Wanting to touch, to kiss, to lose themselves in each other; yet at the same time knowing it wouldn't be sensible.

When they went to the next room Marco took Becca's hand on the way, lacing his fingers through hers. Her skin tingled where he touched her.

Oh, help. This wasn't the deal. She was his therapist, not his girlfriend. South Africa was in the past, and it was staying there.

The study held more bookshelves and a polished oak desk with more family portraits in pride of place.

'This is Papá's, but Ferdy and I use it sometimes if we're here and he's not,' Marco said. 'The next two floors are just bathrooms and bedrooms,' he told her, leading her up the stairs again. 'But this is my favourite bit of the house.'

He led her up a last flight of stairs, released her hand and opened the door for her.

She gasped as she realised what it was. 'A roof garden. How amazing.'

It was stunning—flagged stone, with terracotta pots of sweet-smelling herbs and bright flowers, comfortable chairs and even a hammock. But the bit that took her breath away was the view: not just the whole of the park, but the middle of London itself, including iconic structures such as the London Eye and the Shard.

They were right in the centre of London, with thousands of people around them; and yet at the same time the garden was incredibly private. She assumed that the other houses in the sweeping terrace had some kind of roof gardens, too, but this one didn't seem overlooked in any direction.

'And then there's this. You don't get the same kind of view of the stars that we did in South Africa,' he said, 'because there's too much light pollution in the city, but it's still good to sit out here and look up at the sky on a summer's night.'

'This' referred to a spa pool, screened off from the rest of the garden by a trellis covered in wisteria.

'I thought maybe we could have dinner up here tonight,' he said.

'I've never had dinner on a roof garden before,' Becca said.

'Good. I think you'll enjoy this. Excuse me a second.' He took his mobile phone from his pocket and made a swift call in Spanish.

'Chef would like to know if you have any allergies or if there's anything you don't like?' he asked.

Becca couldn't quite process this. He had a

personal chef? 'No allergies. I'm happy to eat anything.' And then a nasty thought hit her. 'But I'm not keen on puddings with alcohol.'

'That's fine. I'll make sure he knows.' He spoke rapidly into the phone in Spanish again. 'OK, Miguel. *Talué.*'

'What does that mean...*talué*?' she asked.

'It's bye-bye.' He wrinkled his nose. 'Basically it's slang, running the words *"hasta luego"* together. I guess it's like saying *ciao-ciao* in Italian instead of *arrivederci.*'

'Right.' She didn't speak Italian, either, apart from with the aid of a phrasebook.

He grimaced. 'Sorry. I didn't mean to show off. Chef will, though.' He grinned. 'I told him he can show off as much as he likes and do you a real Sirmontanean meal.'

She was still trying to get her head round this. 'You have a personal chef?'

He rolled his eyes. 'You make it sound far more snooty than it is. My parents have to entertain when they're here, and visiting dignitaries kind of expect their full attention rather than having my mother rushing off in the middle of dinner to check something in the kitchen.'

His parents. His family. Ice trickled through her veins. What if his family came over to be with him now he was out of the clinic? Would they think she was suitable to be his physio?

They definitely wouldn't think of her as suitable in any other way.

The panic must have shown in her face, because he sighed. 'Relax, Becca. It's just you and me. My family is under strict instructions to stay away because I need to rest.'

Even though part of her was relieved, part of her felt a bit guilty. 'Isn't that a bit unfair to your mother? She must be worried about you.' In her shoes Becca would have been worried sick and desperate to see her injured son for herself.

Not that Becca thought she'd ever get married and have a family of her own. Her experiences with family had pretty much put her off taking that particular risk.

'I love my mother, I really do, but she drives me totally *loco*,' Marco said. 'She frets and she thinks up all the worst-case scenarios. If she had her way she'd wrap me in cotton wool, and that doesn't sit well with me—and then I end up rebelling and snapping at her, and then she gets upset, and then I feel guilty for being mean because I know she loves me as much as I love her, and...' He grimaced. 'Like I said, *loco*.'

It must be nice, Becca thought, to have a parent who cared that much about you instead of one who always put herself first and dumped you when the going got tough. Not that she had any intention of telling Marco about any of that. She didn't need his pity.

'We should do your physio,' she said.

'So when do I get to do the next stage of exercises?' he asked. 'The ones where I can start doing light work with my hand?'

'The next stage of exercises will be in about another fortnight. And another month after that before you do light activities.'

He groaned. 'Surely I can start using my hand *soon*?'

'Not even to read a newspaper,' she said. 'And using a knife is totally out of the question. That counts as heavy use, and that won't be until three months after the operation. Light use you can start two months after the operation. *Provided* you don't push it and set your progress back before then.'

'Excuse me a second.' He took out his phone and made another call in rapid Spanish.

She gave him an enquiring look.

'I asked Miguel—Chef—to make food I can eat with a fork,' he said, looking grumpy. 'This is worse than being a toddler. I hate the idea of someone cutting up my food for me.' He sighed. 'It's the lack of independence that's getting to me. Not being able to do things I've taken for granted for years.'

'Patience,' she counselled.

'Something I'm not very good at.'

'You were patient with the children in South Africa.'

'That was different.' He shrugged off the compliment. 'Ferdy—now, *he* has patience. Which is why it's so good for Sirmontane that he's the elder son and not me.'

'Do you mind that you won't be king?' she asked.

'No. I have so much more freedom than Ferdy.' He sighed. 'Though obviously I have royal duties. Things I can't neglect. Things that have to come first no matter how I feel about it.'

'It's the same with your hand,' she said lightly. 'You're desperate to use it again—but you have to wait and the healing has to take place first, no matter how grumpy and frustrated you get.'

'Point taken,' he said dryly.

'Time for your exercises.' She talked him through them, watching him and making sure that he didn't push too hard, yet at the same time pushed himself hard enough to make progress.

They were halfway through the physio session when Maria came up onto the roof garden, carrying a tray bearing a silver teapot with a matching jug and sugar bowl, two porcelain cups, and a plate of delicate almond biscuits.

'Miguel's so happy to have you home,

Marco—he's enjoying having someone to cook for other than just the two of us and Rafa,' she said with a smile. 'I'm happy to have you home, too, *hermoso.*'

He smiled at her. 'Thank you, Maria. Though I can assure you that they looked after me well at the Hunter Clinic.'

'It's not Harley Street that worried me,' she said pointedly.

Marco rolled his eyes. 'If Mamá has asked you to nag me about my job, I'll take that as read and you don't have to do it. I'm still in one piece, just a little bit battered, and Becca's fixing me up. She's bullying me, mind.'

Maria laughed and patted Becca's shoulder. 'Bully away, *hermosa.* He needs taking in hand. I brought tea, but if you'd rather have coffee I can bring you some—no problem.'

'Tea's lovely, thank you. It's very kind of you.' Becca smiled at her. 'Though, to be honest, I'd normally make my own tea, and I feel a bit guilty, having you wait on me.'

'Nonsense. That's what I'm here for.' Maria smiled again. 'Call me if you need me.'

'Thank you,' Becca said.

The almond biscuits were lovely.

'These are gorgeous. Can you tell Miguel for me?'

'Sure. They're traditional Sirmontane biscuits,' Marco said. 'They're usually served with coffee after dinner, or sometimes with morning coffee.'

'The tea looks more like an English tradition, though.'

He grinned. 'Yes. Like our neighbours, Spain and France, in Sirmontane we prefer coffee to tea.'

'Just remember you're not to lift anything with your left hand at the moment, even a cup as light and delicate as this,' Becca said, and took charge of the teapot.

Serving tea to a prince, with fine porcelain and silver. If anyone had told her a couple of weeks ago that she'd be doing that she would have laughed. How far away this felt from her real life.

They finished off the physiotherapy session after their tea, and then she was content to sit with Marco in the sunshine and chat about nothing in particular. Just being with him felt so good. And as long as she didn't let herself remember that she was in a multimillion-pound house with a prince, it felt *real*.

Dinner that evening started with tapas. 'Obviously, because we're on the Spanish border, we have similar dishes to Spain,' he said. 'And I like tapas. Lots of little tastes.'

There were dishes of olives, ham, cheeses she didn't recognise but which were totally delicious, and fresh bread. 'This is very nice,' she said, tasting each one in turn.

'And, best of all, I can eat it one-handed,' he said wryly.

The next course was a tender lamb stew, with saffron-scented rice and baby vegetables.

'Fork food at its finest,' Marco said with a grin. 'Miguel's done us proud.'

And then Maria brought up cinnamon-spiked *churros* with the most amazing chocolate sauce.

'Oh, my God. I've never eaten anything as nice as this,' Becca said.

He grinned. 'I told you Sirmontane chocolate's better than Swiss.'

'Lizzie's going to beg you for some of this,' she said, taking another bite.

'I'll get some delivered as a welcome-back present.' Marco laughed.

Finally they had bitter coffee, with the nicest dark chocolate thins she'd ever had in her life, and watched the lights come up over London.

'We could,' Marco suggested softly, 'have a spa bath.'

She shook her head. 'Nice idea, but I'm afraid I don't have a swimming costume with me.' Hers was back in her locker in the clinic.

He pursed his lips. 'What if I said you don't need a costume?'

Oh, the very idea of sharing a spa bath with him—skinny-dipping under the stars… It sent a shiver of desire through her.

'Marco, this—we can't—we shouldn't…' Her voice faded.

'I have no idea what you're trying to tell me, *hermosa*.'

'Oh, yes, you do. I'm your therapist. I can't be anything else.'

He took her hand. 'We're not at the clinic, now. Technically, you're not at work. You're having dinner with me.'

'A platonic dinner.'

'It doesn't have to be.'

'Marco, I'm not going to be just a distraction for you. I'm worth more than that.'

'I know you are.'

But he didn't relinquish her hand. Instead, he raised it very slowly, turned it over so he could see her wrist, and pressed his mouth against her pulse-point. And she knew that he'd be aware of how much her heart-rate was speeding up—and precisely why.

'Remember what I said before?' he whispered. 'Forget the past. Don't worry about the future. Just enjoy the here and now.'

She wanted to. So very badly. It had been

driving her crazy, keeping her distance from him and trying her best to be professional when all she wanted to do was rip his clothes off.

But…

'How can I?' she burst out.

'Becca,' he said, 'will you please just shut up and kiss me?'

She narrowed her eyes at him. 'Is that an order, Your Royal Highness?'

'No. It's a polite request. And I did say "please",' he pointed out. 'Or do you want me to beg?'

Oh, help. The pictures *that* put in her head. She dragged in a breath. 'I know I'm technically off duty, but you're still my patient.'

'Then consider me signed off, as of now,' he said.

'I'm afraid I can't do that. Only Ethan can sign you off, as your surgeon. Or maybe Declan, as the acting head of the clinic. And you'd be stupid to sign yourself off. Your hand…'

He groaned. 'Right now I don't care about my hand. This is driving me crazy, Becca. I can't stop thinking about you.'

The confession seemed dragged from him, and it made it easier for her to admit to him, 'I can't stop thinking about you, either.'

'I need to be honest with you. I'm not sure I can offer you a happy-ever-after. I have…well, responsibilities. I still have to finish my tour of duty as a soldier. How do I know that the next bomb won't be directly under my Jeep instead of the one in front of mine?'

'Marco.' She stroked his face. 'Don't talk like that.' She hated to think of him being badly hurt, or even killed.

'I'm not trying to manipulate you, Becca, or bully you into having a fling with me.'

'Is that what you're offering? A fling?'

He blew out a breath. 'Right now it's all I can offer. Maybe—I don't know. Maybe. I don't want to make any promises I can't keep. That wouldn't be fair to either of us. But I can offer you happy-for-now.'

Was that enough?

Either way, she knew that he was going to walk out of her life in a few weeks' time.

If she said no, all she would have were regrets. In years to come, would she wish that she'd been brave?

If she said yes, they could have some time together. Build memories. Things that might sustain her and might just stop her spiralling back into addiction again when he left.

'Seize the day,' she said softly, and leaned forward to kiss him.

How good his skin felt under her fingertips. How good his mouth felt as it teased hers, tempted her, incited her to bite his lower lip and kiss him back.

Despite only having one working hand, it took him seconds to loosen her hair.

'That's what I wanted to see,' he said softly. 'Your hair falling over your shoulders, just like it used to. Fire over cream.'

Oh, God. How had she forgotten how damn sexy he was? Even the way he talked to her made her feel wet. Hot. Needy. Nobody else had ever made her feel this way. It had been so easy to refuse dates, because the men in question hadn't made her feel a fraction of what Marco made her feel.

He brushed a kiss against her mouth. 'Becca. I want to sit with you and drink champagne and look at the stars—well, as much as you get to see of the stars in London.'

'You're on antibiotics,' she pointed out, 'so that's not a good idea.'

'OK. You can drink champagne and I'll watch you,' he said.

Oh, help. She didn't want to explain all this. She didn't drink. Ever. She couldn't risk even one sip in case it pushed her straight back down the slope of addiction. 'No, it's fine. I'm not one for champagne,' she said hastily.

'Pimm's, then?' he suggested. 'Or a cocktail? Miguel makes wicked cocktails.'

Worse and worse. It looked as if Becca was going to have to tell him a certain amount. But she had no intention of letting him push her into a more detailed explanation. 'Actually, I don't drink,' she said. 'Sorry.'

Marco looked intrigued.

The only way she could think of to take his mind off the subject and stop him asking questions was to kiss him. And she was quivering by the time Marco broke the kiss.

'Let's get in the pool,' he said.

'You're not going anywhere near that water without a plastic bag over your arm. You can't get the splint wet. Or the dressing.'

He laughed. 'You're so bossy.'

'Someone has to be. Right now you're exuberant, bored, and full of bright ideas,' she said.

He kissed her lightly. 'Guilty on all three counts. But my bright ideas are great.'

'Another day,' she said. 'When I can make sure I tape up your arm properly and I have something to wear.'

'I'll hold you to that,' he said, and the expression in his eyes made desire lick all the way down her spine. 'OK. Second bright idea. How about you stay here tonight? I remember what it was like, waking up with you in my arms. It might be nice to do that in a comfortable bed instead of a sleeping bag.'

Becca was tempted. Deeply tempted. Though she knew it was a bad idea. The closer she let him get now, the more she was in danger of getting in too deep and ending up hurt again. Making love with him would be one thing; but allowing him a deeper intimacy, like she had in South Africa—that was one risk too far.

'I don't have so much as a toothbrush with me.'

'Not a problem. Our guest bathrooms are well stocked.'

'I don't have any clean clothes, either.'

'Maria can laund—'

She stopped him by pressing one finger gently against his lips. 'Marco, I'm not used to this way of life. I don't have staff. I've always looked after myself. I'm not comfortable with making other people clear up after me. And I don't expect anyone else to launder my clothes for me.' Colour crept into her face. 'Plus…I don't want her to think…well.'

'That you're my lover?' He raised an eyebrow. 'Maria's a woman of the world. Married, too. You've probably guessed that Miguel's her husband. And, despite me teasing her earlier, she's not my mother's spy. She's the soul of discretion. She's been with my family for years— since before I was born.'

'Was she the nanny you told me about?'

He smiled. 'Yes.'

That certainly explained Maria's easy relationship with the Prince and the way she teased him and fussed over him.

'I just feel awkward about it, Marco,' she said.

'OK. So how about,' he said, 'I see you tomorrow—you stay for dinner and bring a swimming costume with you?'

She bit her lip. 'I need to be somewhere tomorrow evening.' To do the volunteer shift she'd skipped tonight.

He stroked her face. 'I don't want you thinking I'm just bored and using you to distract me. Because I'm not. I want to be with you, Becca.'

It was so very tempting.

'I'll sort it out,' she said. He wouldn't be in London for much longer. She'd make the most of the time they had together. 'But I need to go now, Marco.'

'I'll ask Rafa to drive you home in the limo.'

She shook her head. 'I don't need a limo. I'll get the tube. The station's not far from here.'

He sighed. 'I'm not trying to control you, you know. I just want to make things easier for you.'

'I'm fine.' She smiled. 'Don't fuss. I'll see you tomorrow.'

'Mañana,' Marco said, and kissed her, tak-

ing his time and heating her blood to the point that she almost, *almost* changed her mind and agreed to stay.

'I'll see you out.'

As Marco closed the front door behind Becca, so he didn't have to watch her walk away, he knew she was right. If a limo with blacked-out glass took her home the neighbours would ask questions, maybe start talking. A word to the press here, a car number plate given there, and connections would soon be made.

He needed to keep his links with her out of the public eye and out of the press. Not because he was ashamed of her—of course he wasn't. She'd always been cagey about her own background, and had been even cagier since she'd discovered he was a prince, so he was guessing that she came from a very modest family. But money didn't bother him. It was how people treated others that mattered to him. You could be as high-born as you like and still be a low-life.

No, he wasn't ashamed of her. It was what the press could do if they found out about her that bothered him. He'd seen for himself how easily the press could hurt people—how public criticism had chipped away at the confidence of his sister-in-law-to-be Marianna. He didn't want that to happen to Becca. So keeping her secret would be the best thing he could do for both of them.

CHAPTER SEVEN

MARCO FOUND HIMSELF looking forward to seeing Becca, and he loved the fact that she'd talk to him about everything under the sun. Except one thing: she was seriously secretive about her past. She changed the subject every time he asked a question about her. He knew absolutely nothing about her family—were her parents still together, still alive?

'You're a puzzle,' he said.

She frowned. 'I'm not with you.'

'I know nothing about you.'

'There's nothing much to know.' She shrugged. 'I'm a physiotherapist, I specialise in treating hands, and that's about it.'

'So this thing in the evenings that you do—is it a course? You mentioned that you were thinking about studying acupuncture.'

'No, I'm not studying acupuncture yet—I'm still in the process of choosing a course.'

He noticed that she'd switched the subject

again, and she hadn't told him what she was doing in the evenings. Why wouldn't she open up to him? Did she think he'd hurt her? And how could he get her to trust him?

Though at the same time he knew she was right: he couldn't offer her a future because his duty to his family and his country had to come first.

Yet he needed her.

And he thought that she might need him.

Somehow they'd manage to find a way to make this work.

Somehow.

'I can't stay for dinner, but is the offer of the spa pool still open?' Becca asked, later that day.

'It most certainly is—OK, so it means we don't get to see the very few stars you can see in the London night sky, but we can watch the clouds going past instead. How about after lunch?' he suggested.

'That'd be great.' She gave him a shy smile that left him tingling. 'I brought my costume with me. And a bag for your arm, and tape.'

'That's good.'

'But, for now...'

'I know, I know,' he said. 'Exercises.'

In the middle of the afternoon Marco changed into his swimming trunks and Becca taped up his arm to make sure that his splint wouldn't get wet. He climbed into the pool and settled back next to her with a contented sigh.

'This,' he said, 'is paradise. I love London.'

'Wouldn't you rather be in Sirmontane, in the mountains?' she asked.

'Not when I can't ride a bike or go skiing,' he said wryly. 'Of course I love my country, but there's something special for me about London. There's music, there's drama, there are museums and art galleries—you can eat foods from practically any country in the world, walk in the park, dance in the middle of a fountain. . .'

'Well, *you* can't dance in the middle of a fountain—not unless you bag your arm up like that, and I think that might cramp your style a bit,' she teased.

He laughed, pulled her close with his good arm and kissed her. 'I don't think it cramps my style at all.'

'No?' she teased.

God, he couldn't resist her. 'No.' His expression grew hot, and this time his kiss wasn't all sweetness and gentleness. It was demanding and enticing and promising, all at the same time. He needed her to know how he felt. Needed her to feel the same way.

Nobody else had ever made Becca feel this way—as if she were going up in flames every time his skin touched hers. It had been so easy to refuse dates because the men in question hadn't made her feel a thousandth of what Marco made her feel.

'I need to see you, Becca,' Marco said, tracing the edge of her swimming costume with the tip of his forefinger. 'And nobody's going to interrupt us. This is just you and me.'

She couldn't resist him any more. 'Yes,' she whispered.

It took him a second to slide the straps down her shoulders. And then he was cupping one breast, his thumb stroking her nipple and making her gasp.

He dipped his head and took her nipple into his mouth.

Becca shuddered as he sucked. 'Oh, my God.' It had been way too long since she'd felt anything like that. Since she'd let anyone touch her in this way. And how strange it was that they were both older, changed by their experiences—and yet their bodies reacted the same way they always had.

'You like that?' he asked.

'Yes,' she breathed.

'Good.' He stroked her abdomen and she knelt up, arching against him.

'I'd forgotten how good we are together,' he whispered. 'How you feel. Like warm silk.'

He slid one finger underneath the lower hem of her swimsuit and drew it along the length of her sex. The second time he did it she was quivering. And when he pushed a finger deep into her, she was glad that he'd jammed his mouth over hers again because she couldn't help whimpering in sheer need.

All coherence left her as her body began to tighten round him.

'Better?' he asked softly when she'd come back down to earth.

She felt the colour flood into her face.

He simply grinned. 'It's good to know that it's still like that between us.'

'I…' She shook her head. 'I don't know what to say.'

He kissed her softly. 'Then don't say anything.'

But she didn't want him thinking that she was cheap. Because she wasn't. 'I don't normally do this sort of thing.'

'Neither do I,' Marco said dryly, 'no matter what the press like to think.' Then he frowned. 'Are you telling me you haven't made love with anyone else since we were together?'

'No.'

Guilt flooded through him. 'Because of me?'

'Partly,' she said, but he had a feeling that she was trying to let him off the hook.

'I hurt you that much?'

She shrugged. 'I was young. I guess we both were. And in a way you did me a favour. It meant that I concentrated on my studies instead of letting someone distract me.'

Even so, he'd hurt her to the point where she hadn't trusted anyone else. Maybe she'd dated, but she hadn't let her boyfriends go anywhere near this far.

'I'm sorry,' he said. 'I didn't mean to hurt you.' And wasn't he in danger of doing that all over again? Only offering her the here and now? He dragged in a breath. 'Becca, I…'

'"Seize the day", you said.'

'But that isn't who you are. You're careful. Guarded.'

'Now who's overthinking it?'

Her tone was light, but he was sure she was masking something.

How was he going to persuade her to trust him with the rest of her, not just her body? When they made love they were on the same page. But Marco knew that wasn't enough.

'I have to go,' she said.

He wasn't so sure that she really needed to go, but he also knew if he pushed her now he'd lose any chance of getting close to her and really finding out what was in her head.

'OK. I'm not going to push you.' He paused. 'Will you stay for dinner tomorrow?'

'I'll see what I can do.'

'And maybe,' he said, 'you could stay over.' At the panicky look on her face, he said, 'No pressure. You can stay in one of the guest suites, if you prefer.'

Though he really wanted to spend the night with her in his arms. He wanted to wake up with her and know that the day would be better because she was in it. Or maybe he was asking too much.

'I'll see,' she said, and left to do whatever mysterious thing she did in the evenings.

The next morning, doing the limited exercises he was allowed to do in the gym was a form of torture, Marco decided. So was sitting in the library. Usually it was his favourite room in the house, but not when the guitars he couldn't play right now were in full view, reminding him just how limited his movements were.

The only bright spot in his day was the fact that Becca would be spending it with him; and there might be a chance that she would stay for dinner as on the first night.

Whether he could persuade her to stay overnight was another matter. She'd been reluctant, the night before, and she kept mentioning these mysterious commitments, but clammed up if he asked her about them.

He could put tabs on her easily enough, and find out what she did that way. But having her followed like that would feel wrong. He'd much rather she told him herself, of her own free will.

Clearly she didn't trust him. Now he'd got to know her again he could understand why. He'd left her before, in South Africa, not wanting to explain because everything was too complicated. And he'd been too young and thoughtless to realise just how much that had hurt her.

Now they were both older. Wiser, maybe.

Except Marco knew he was in danger of really losing his heart to her. He liked the woman Becca had become—kind, yet at the same time efficient and good at her job.

If only she'd been born royal. Then it would have been so easy for both of them.

It had always been made clear to him that he had a responsibility to his country. That he should marry royalty and consolidate his country's relationship with that of another country. Royal marriages were based on duty first: respect and love had to learn to grow later.

With Ferdy being engaged to Princess Marianna, it had taken the heat off Marco; but Marco also knew that it wouldn't be too long before the pressure was back. Especially as this tour of duty with the army was likely to be his last.

Whatever this thing was between him and Becca, it couldn't last. He'd have to give her up. Even though it would feel like ripping part of himself away.

Marco seemed thrilled when Becca told him that she could stay for dinner. And even more thrilled when, just after lunch, she mentioned that she'd brought an overnight bag with her.

'You're really going to stay?'

'If the offer's still there.'

He kissed her soundly. 'It is. Though I meant what I said about no pressure. You don't have to spend the night in my bed.'

She felt the colour flood into her face. 'What if I want to?' she whispered.

His eyes went really dark and he caught her lower lip between his. 'That,' he said huskily, 'would be a bonus.'

She'd already noticed that his accent changed when he was excited; he sounded much less English and much more Spanish.

Right now, she really wished he had two good arms. She loved the idea of him carrying her to his bed. And she had a feeling that he'd like that idea very much, too.

'Exercises,' she said, more to calm herself

down than anything else. Marco tempted her too much.

'Sure.'

But she noticed he winced slightly.

'Let me see,' she said, and checked his palm. 'If that gets any redder over today, you're going back into the clinic to let Ethan have a look at it, and the paparazzi can do what they like,' she said.

'You think it's infected?'

'I think,' she said, 'we need to be careful.'

And not just with the condition of his hand.

He lay with his head in her lap while she massaged cream into his hand, taking care to be gentle enough not to hurt him yet firm enough to make a difference to the sore, tight skin.

'Thank you,' he said softly when she'd finished, and pressed a kiss to the tips of her fingers.

'Any time,' she said, stroking his cheek.

Even without Marco carrying her to his bed, Becca found herself swept away by the whole romance of sleeping with him. This time it was nothing to do with canvas and a slightly lumpy sleeping bag and everything to do with a four-poster bed, the softest and deepest pillows she'd ever seen, and cool cotton sheets with a thread count so high that the material felt softer than silk.

And, more to the point, she'd brought condoms. So this time they could really make love. Recapture the old closeness.

'I can't stop thinking about you, Becca,' he said, the admission ripping from him. 'About us. And it's driving me crazy.'

In answer, she leaned forward, just far enough to touch her mouth to his. Gently, softly. It started out all sweet and reassuring, but Marco wrapped his good arm around her, drawing her closer, and the kiss spiralled into hot, aching need.

She wasn't sure who started undressing whom, or how much help she gave him, but it seemed to take seconds until they were both naked.

'Do you have any idea how lovely you are?' he asked huskily.

She felt the colour bloom in her cheeks. 'I'm ordinary.'

He stole a kiss. 'Your judgement's off. There's nothing ordinary about you. You're beautiful, Becca.'

'You're not so shabby, yourself.' Her voice sounded husky to her own ears.

Marco traced the line of Becca's collarbones with his fingertips; she shivered, arching her back and tipping her head so he could kiss the hollow of her throat.

He needed her so much. He wanted to touch her. Taste her. Make her feel as desperate as he did.

She shivered. 'Marco…'

He wanted her all wide-eyed and flushed with passion. Like she'd been when he'd touched her in the spa pool. When she'd fallen apart in his arms.

'I'm having a hard time taking this slowly,' he warned.

She traced his pectorals with the tip of her forefinger. 'Me, too.'

'Good.' He was so dizzy with need for her, he couldn't think straight. 'I'm in your hands,' he whispered. 'All yours.'

'All mine,' she repeated, and her mouth and eyes turned so sensual that he caught his breath.

She smoothed her hands across his bare chest and the pads of her fingertips teased his skin, making him ache. He wanted more. Much more.

She leaned forward and pressed a hot, open-mouthed kiss against his throat; he arched his head back, giving her better access, and closed his eyes in bliss as she nibbled her way across his skin. God, her mouth felt so good. And he wanted her to dip lower. To take him into her mouth and ease the ache.

Her hands stroked over his pecs, his abdomen. 'You're gorgeous.'

'And I'm aching for you.'

'Are you, now?' She looked incredibly pleased with herself. 'I need you to put that sling back on. Your hand needs support.'

He couldn't help groaning with impatience. 'You drive me crazy.'

'Oh, I intend to,' she said, her voice husky and making his pulse kick up a notch. 'But I don't want you undoing all the hard work we've put in so far. Sling. *Now*.'

He sighed, and let her put the sling back in place. 'I could really do with two hands to do what I want to do with you.'

'Tough. You've got one. Improvise,' she said, giving him a wicked look from under her lashes.

Slowly, slowly, he dropped to his knees, stroking her abdomen. 'You feel nice.' He moved closer and nuzzled her skin. 'You smell nice.' He traced a circle round her navel with the tip of his tongue. 'And you—' He was aware that she was shaking, and stopped. 'What?'

'I'm trying to work out if you're doing the three monkeys or the three bears.' Her eyes were lit with amusement.

She'd been *laughing*?

'That was supposed to be sexy,' he said, giving her a pained look.

She just laughed at him. 'You should've worn the domino, Zorro,' she teased.

'You like the idea of being seduced by a masked hero?' he asked.

She stopped laughing then and caught her breath. And then she traced his lower lip with the tip of her index finger.

He moved to catch her finger between his lips and sucked. Hard.

'Ohhh.' It was a high, breathy sound. Sheer desire. And his whole body responded to it.

He kissed her throat, nuzzled the hollows of her collarbones; she quivered 'Your *hand*,' she said, looking at him and then looking at the bed.

'Then I guess you get to be in charge,' he said, and pulled back the covers and lay back against the pillows.

She swallowed hard, then retrieved a condom.

'Marco, I…haven't done this for a while,' she said.

'It doesn't matter.' But he was glad she'd reminded him. So he could hold himself back, take it slowly for her. Make sure that she was ready for him. 'Come here.'

Looking suddenly as shy as she had all those years ago, the very first time they'd done this, she walked over to the bed. Sat down.

He sat up again and stroked her face. 'Stop worrying,' he whispered. 'I think we both need this.'

'Yes.' Her green eyes were huge.

He kissed her, very slowly, lingering until he felt her breathing change. And then he lay back, drawing her with him.

She straddled him, and he could feel the heat of her sex against his skin.

'Now?' he whispered.

'Now.' She rolled on the condom with shaking hands, then slowly eased herself down on him.

This felt perfect. 'You feel amazing,' he whispered, pushing deeper. 'It's like the very first time.'

'Yeah.'

Her voice sounded shaky. Was she crying? He stopped moving and shifted slightly so he could look her in the eye.

'Are you OK?' he asked softly. 'Really OK?'

She nodded, clearly not trusting herself to speak.

'If you want me to stop, Becca, then I'll stop. It's fine to change your mind.' He touched her cheek with the backs of his fingers.

'It's just—it's been a while for me. And I wasn't expecting...' Her voice trailed off.

'Neither was I,' he said. And although he wanted her, very badly, he knew she needed reassurance before anything else could happen. 'Do you want me to stop?' he asked quietly.

She shook her head. 'I don't want you to stop.'

'I don't want to stop, either.' He lowered his mouth to hers in a warm, sweet, reassuring kiss. He could feel the softness of her breasts against his skin, the hardness of her nipples—and he loved being wrapped in her warm, sweet depths.

Pleasure spiralled through him and he slowed everything right down, focusing on the pleasure; he could tell it was the same for her because she gasped and bore down on him, letting him push deeper.

And then he felt her body tighten round his, pushing him into his own climax—and it was sweeter than anything he could ever remember. Sweeter than even their first time. It felt as if he'd just found something he hadn't even known was missing—but now he knew what it was he was complete.

'My Becca,' he whispered, and sat up so he could wrap his good arm round her and hold her close.

She rested her forehead against his shoulder. 'Marco.'

They just stayed together for a while, holding each other close, enjoying the closeness. And then finally he said softly, 'I need to deal with the condom. But I'm telling you now: I want to go to sleep with you in my arms. I need you close.'

'That's fine by me,' she said softly.

* * *

Becca woke the next morning, curled against Marco's side. He was lying on his back and her head was resting on his right shoulder. She gently eased herself away so she didn't wake him, and propped herself on one elbow so she could watch him sleeping.

Asleep, relaxed, he was beautiful—and he was all hers. She didn't have to share him with anyone. It was better even than in South Africa, because there they'd both been busy and had been needed by other people; here it was just the two of them in their own little bubble.

She knew it was going to end and she ought to keep her heart more guarded, but at the same time she knew she still loved him. She needed to be with him for as long as she could.

If only things could have been different. If only she'd had a different life growing up. Maybe if her past had been squeaky clean his family might be able to overlook the fact that she didn't have royal blood—but her past was far from squeaky clean. She'd been in a rehab clinic at sixteen. And you couldn't change the past—you could only do your best to hide it.

Later that day, Becca noticed Maria wincing in pain as she put the tray on the table.

'Maria, would you sit down for a moment, please?' she asked.

The housekeeper looked slightly worried. 'Is there a problem? Something wrong?'

'I think that's what you could tell me,' Becca said gently. 'Remember what I do for a living—OK, I'm a hand specialist, but before I specialised I learned about the rest of the body's systems, and I think right now you're in pain.'

Maria gave a dismissive flap of her hand. 'It doesn't matter. This sort of thing happens when you get older.'

'Arthritis?' Becca guessed.

'My hip. And the tablets don't work as well as they used to,' Maria admitted. 'Maybe I should go back to the doctor and see if he can give me something else. But, please—don't tell Marco. I don't want the family to think I can't do my job and pension me off. I love working here.'

'Marco's in the gym and, knowing him, he'll be there for a while,' Becca said. 'If you wouldn't mind me examining you, I might be able to give you some exercises to help with the pain.'

'Really?'

'Really. One of my favourite patients has arthritic hands. I give her exercises to help with the mobility and the pain, and I've seen a big difference over the last six months. I can do the same for you.'

Maria looked close to tears. 'That's so kind of you, *hermosa*.'

'It's the least I can do, seeing how you've spoiled me since I've been here,' Becca said.

Gently, she examined the older woman, getting her to go through a range of movements so she could see where the trouble spots were. She'd just finished teaching Maria some exercises when Marco came back into the room.

'Good morning, Maria,' he said. 'Am I too late for coffee?'

'It's cold now. I'll get you some more,' Maria said.

'It's my fault. I made her sit down and talk to me,' Becca said with a smile. 'She's told me loads of scurrilous stories about you as a child.'

'I was a perfect child,' Marco protested, laughing.

'A perfect monster, yeah,' Becca teased. 'You told me yourself how your mum had to apologise for you all the time. Making little princesses kiss your pet frog.'

'I didn't make them kiss my pet frog. I just put him on the chair next to them.' He grinned. 'They were annoying. And it stopped them pestering me to play dressing-up games when I would rather have been climbing trees.'

Maria laughed. 'He was a bit of a tearaway.'

When Maria had left, she looked at Marco. 'Can I talk to you about something?'

'Sure.'

'And it won't go any further than you?'

He frowned. 'What's wrong?'

'I need that promise first.'

'OK. I promise.'

'Thank you. There's just something I've noticed. Maria doesn't have a lot of help, and her job's physically quite demanding.'

He looked at her. 'Are you saying this with your work hat on?'

'Pointing out that some work systems might need improving? Yes,' she said. 'Though don't you *dare* say a word to Maria.'

'Patient confidentiality?' he asked softly.

'I,' Becca said crisply, 'am not answering that. But I was just thinking there must be a way to make things a bit easier for her, but doing it tactfully, so she doesn't feel that you all think she's no longer competent.'

'I think,' Marco said, 'I get what you're saying—and also what you're not saying. And, yes, in that case, we need to be tactful. She's been with the family since Ferdy was a baby. She's part of us. That's not ever going to change and I'll make sure she knows it. But I agree, she needs more help. I should have noticed.'

'Why would you notice? You're a prince.'

'I'm a soldier,' he corrected. 'And I look at systems all the time. How things work. I should take more notice in my own home instead of being complacent and thinking that this is the way we've always done things, so this is the way it's always going to be. I'll talk to Mamá and get it sorted.'

'Good.'

'That's teamwork,' Marco said, and gave her a high five with his right hand.

'Talking of work,' Becca said, 'now you've finished being a gym rat, time to do your hand exercises.'

'Yes, boss,' Marco teased, and let her release the hand strap on his splint.

Whatever Becca's mysterious commitments were, she'd clearly managed to change her schedule because she actually agreed to stay overnight every night for the next week. Though Marco noticed that she insisted on going home before dinner and doing her own laundry. Although in some respects it annoyed him, because it was so unnecessary, at the same time he liked Becca's sense of independence and the fact that she wasn't afraid to say no to him.

It made him realise that he was falling more and more deeply in love with her. And that wasn't fair to either of them, because he still hadn't worked out how he could fit her into his life along with his royal duties.

Or maybe, he thought, he was just getting a bit stir-crazy at being cooped up here. Maybe they needed to go out and escape all the worries and just have a bit of fun. It couldn't be somewhere too public, because they'd be caught on a camera lens, but he knew somewhere they could go.'

'Tomorrow night,' he said, 'let's go dancing.'

She looked surprised, then wary. 'Dancing?'

'At a club.'

'But—isn't that a bit, well, public?'

'It's an exclusive club in Soho, owned by friends of mine.' He smiled. 'Mardi's. Short for Mardi Gras—they play mainly Latin music. Samba, salsa, tango.'

'Your kind of music?' she guessed.

'Absolutely. And it's somewhere that our privacy will be respected, because my friends will be careful for us.'

She smiled. 'You're asking me out on a date, Prince Marco?'

He shrugged. 'If you like.'

'You and I—we've never been on a date,' she said thoughtfully. 'Not even in South Africa.'

'Then maybe it's time we did.'

She bit her lip. 'Marco, we…'

He pressed the tip of his forefinger to her mouth, very gently. 'I know. But we agreed— we'll live for the moment. And I want to dance with you, Becca.'

She looked thrilled. And then wary again. 'I, um, don't really do clubs normally. So, um, I don't think I have anything suitable to wear.'

'That's easily sorted. What size are you?'

He eyes widened. 'What?'

'What size are your shoes, your clothes?'

'No way am I going to wear a dress that one of your women left behind,' she said, sounding disgusted.

He laughed. 'I wouldn't insult you by suggesting anything like that. Apart from the fact that I don't normally bring women here, the only women within twenty years of your age who leave stuff here are my sister Bella or Ferdy's fiancée Marianna. Although they're both about the same size as you, their styles aren't the same as yours.'

'Uh-huh.'

'And, just for the record, the press exaggerates hugely. I don't date anywhere near as much as they like to make out, and I'm quite picky about who I sleep with, too.'

'Sorry.' She sighed. 'I'm not good at this relationship business.'

'Neither am I,' he said softly. 'I've made my

share of mistakes. Look at what happened when I rescued my men. I made the most stupid tactical error. And other people paid for that.'

Mistakes.

This was her cue to tell him about the massive ones she'd made.

But she knew that if she told him the truth about her past, he'd start to despise her. Besides, she'd moved on from those grim, dark days. It was better to keep her own counsel.

'I'll sort you out something to wear,' he said. 'I need your dress size and your shoe size.'

'So, what? We find something on the internet and you get the stuff delivered here?'

'Better than that,' he said with a grin. 'Leave this with me.'

It wasn't until the next morning that she discovered what he meant, when Maria showed a couple of men holding armfuls of bags into the sitting room.

'Your Highness—I hope we've come up with a selection you'll like,' the first man said, bowing.

Marco had organised a shop to come to them?

And then Becca recognised the logo on the bags. A luxury department store. A place where the celebrity clients of the Harley Street clinic all had accounts, no doubt, but it was way out of Becca's league. She was too stunned to say a word.

'I'm sure you've covered everything,' Marco said with a smile. 'Thank you for being so accommodating. As you can see, I'd find shopping a little tricky at the moment.' He indicated his strapped-up hand.

'We're always happy to help, Your Highness,' the man said. 'Shall we call by this afternoon to collect what didn't suit?'

'That would be perfect. Thank you so much.'

No wonder the newspapers called him Prince Charming. Because he was.

When the shop's staff had left, Becca sat down on one of the sofas. 'Marco, please don't think I'm ungrateful, but I wasn't expecting this. I'm afraid my salary doesn't run to designer originals.'

'It doesn't have to. This was my idea, so it's my bill.'

She frowned. 'I don't expect you to buy my clothes, Marco.'

'Becca, this isn't about being a control freak and telling you what to do—I just wanted to do something nice for you, buy you a dress and shoes so we can go dancing. Is that so very bad?'

She grimaced. 'Sorry. Now I feel like a spoiled brat having a tantrum.'

He laughed. 'Trust me, I've seen spoiled women having a tantrum—and that didn't even come close.'

'It just feels weird, having a shop come to me instead of the other way round.'

'My mother and my sister do this all the time,' he said.

'Royal privilege?'

'More like valued customer privilege—they spend a lot of money at this particular store, and the store looks after them so they don't take their custom to a different store. Either they get stuff brought here, or the store opens for them outside normal shopping hours so they can go shopping in peace. I'm pretty sure they do that for other customers who spend a lot of money with them, too.'

'I guess,' Becca said, still feeling awkward.

He shrugged. 'If it makes you feel better, this way it's safer for me—if we go shopping in actual shops, supposing someone knocks into me and damages my hand?'

She coughed. 'Right, and that's not going to happen at all if we go dancing tonight?'

'It's not,' he said, 'because we're going to a small and fairly exclusive club.'

The one owned by his friends. No doubt from the moneyed set. Where she wouldn't fit in.

As if he guessed her fears, he said softly,

'Becca. This is just you and me, getting away from it all for an evening. Besides, I loathe shopping. I hate dragging round the shops. The chances are there will be someone tailing me in the hope of getting a story, and would you really want pictures of any underwear you bought splashed all over the tabloids, along with a lot of speculation?'

She'd hate being in the spotlight. And the idea of the press finding out anything about her made her bone-deep terrified. 'No.'

'Come on. Let's have a look at what they brought.'

The bags contained dresses, underwear, shoes, and accessories—in lots of different styles and colours. 'This is amazing.'

'So do I get a fashion show?' he asked.

She raised an eyebrow. 'Does this mean you're going to choose my dress?'

'No, *you're* going to choose the dress, but I want the fun of seeing you in every single one of them.'

Becca was surprised to discover just how much fun it was, dressing up and walking up and down the sitting room while Marco looked on thoughtfully.

Finally she chose a classic little black dress, shoes that were high enough to be elegant and yet low enough to dance in, and a small evening bag that was just big enough to contain her phone, keys, and some money.

'There's something missing,' he said. 'Ah, here we go.' He took a pile of boxes from another bag and started opening them. 'Diamonds—no, they're cold and you're all about warmth.' He opened another box. 'How about this set of black pearls? Look at the lustre; you can see your reflection in them.'

Diamonds and pearls? This didn't seem real. Becca rarely wore jewellery, but when she did it was costume jewellery.

Then Marco opened another box. 'No, this is the one. Just like your eyes.' He held up an emerald choker.

A chill ran through her. 'Aren't emeralds supposed to be unlucky?'

'No. That's just because they're more fragile than other stones and are more likely to chip.'

She narrowed her eyes at him. 'And how do you know so much about jewellery?'

'I had a misspent youth.' He grinned. 'OK, my grandmother has a few emerald pieces and she told me.'

Again, Becca was reminded of the differences between them. Nobody in her family had ever had jewellery, let alone 'a few emerald pieces'. As far as Becca knew, her mother had pawned her engagement ring and wedding ring so she could spend the money on alcohol.

She pushed the thought away. They'd agreed to live for the moment. And this was a night out at an exclusive club where they'd be safe from the crowds. 'Thank you.'

CHAPTER EIGHT

THAT EVENING, WHEN Becca emerged from the bathroom with her hair pinned up and the emerald choker round her neck, Marco looked at her, his eyes widening.

'You look stunning. Not that you don't look beautiful every day,' he added swiftly, 'but I've never seen you all dressed up to go out before. That dress suits you.'

'Thank you.'

'I've been thinking—it's probably easiest if I go first, then send Rafa back for you.'

She frowned. 'Why are we going separately?'

He grimaced. 'Because it's easier.'

'How? We're leaving from the same place and going to the same place, so it makes sense to share the transport.' Then understanding dawned. 'Marco, you said we were going dancing—on a real date. Have you changed your mind? Am I not good enough to be seen with you in public?'

'It's nothing to do with that.' He sighed. 'Look, my life is pretty much like a goldfish bowl. There was a media blanket when I was in Afghanistan but it's back to the usual free-for-all now. I just want to spare you from that.'

She went cold. Did he know about her past? Had he found out, somehow? His family's security team had probably investigated her and discovered the truth.

'It's just not much fun being hounded by the press, that's all,' he said softly. 'I've seen how much it's knocked Marianna's confidence. I guess I'm trying to protect you.'

So maybe he *didn't* know the truth about her, then. She just prayed she could keep her secrets until their fling was over.

'I'll go first, then meet you in there. Rafa will drive you,' he said, and kissed her swiftly. 'You look lovely. And I can't wait to go dancing with you. See you shortly.'

Was this the right thing to do? Becca wondered. Plus it would be really intimidating, meeting him in a strange place where he knew everyone but she would know nobody.

But Marco had been getting twitchy for the last couple of days. Maybe it would settle him, seeing his friends.

She went to chat with Maria in the kitchen while Rafa drove Marco to the club.

'Look at you, *hermosa*! Gorgeous,' Maria said, resting her hands on Becca's shoulders and looking at her.

'Thank you.'

'You're good for Marco, you know,' Maria said. 'Not like those fluffy women who chatter on about nothing and only care about their clothes.'

If only. Becca wrinkled her nose. 'I'm not under any illusions that it's going to last, Maria. I'm not from the right background.'

'Love always finds a way,' Maria said. 'And you love him, don't you?'

'I've loved him for years,' Becca admitted. 'I never got over him when he left me last time.'

'This time,' Maria said, 'it will be different.'

Becca knew it wouldn't be—how could there possibly be a happy ending for her and Marco when they came from such different worlds?—but she smiled at the older woman and pretended to agree.

Then Rafa came into the kitchen. 'I'll take you to the Prince,' he said.

Becca baulked when he opened the door at the back for her. 'Would you mind very much if I sat with you, instead?'

'It's a scary lifestyle the Prince leads, yes?'

Rafa smiled at her. 'Sure, come and sit with me. I don't mind.'

He drove her to Soho and parked just outside the club.

'Are you going to be all right? Would you like me to walk you in?' he asked.

'No, I'm just being pathetic. I'll be fine. But thank you for being kind, Rafa.'

'No problem, *señorita*. Have a good time and I'll see you when you're ready to go home.'

She nodded. 'Marco will ring you?'

Rafa smiled. 'I wait here until you're ready.' Clearly he could see that she was about to protest that he shouldn't have to hang around, because he said gently, 'I have the radio for company. It's fine.'

'Then thank you. I'll see you later.'

She walked up the stairs to Mardi's and took a deep breath. It was ridiculous to feel so nervous; but at the same time she knew that she didn't fit into Marco's world.

He'd said the club was owned by friends of his. She hoped that they would at least be polite to her on the surface, for his sake. It would be awful if they were mean and sneered at her.

She took another deep breath and pushed the door open.

The club was amazing. From outside it was a nondescript building, but inside the walls were painted a deep burgundy, and there were fairy lights everywhere. It made the place look magical.

There was a band playing on the small stage—a singer with a guitar, another guitarist, a double bassist and a drummer—and people were dancing. The floor was shiny black with lots of tiny lights set into it so people could see their feet as they danced.

She scanned the room, looking for Marco. He was over by the bar; he lifted his good arm in greeting, and she nerved herself to walk over to him, knowing that the people standing with him would be scrutinising her.

'Good evening, Becca,' he said softly, and kissed her. 'I did wonder if you'd chicken out.'

She shook her head. 'I couldn't do that—what if you knocked your arm and needed urgent physio?'

He laughed. 'No, I just need you.' He stroked her face. 'Come and meet my friends. This is Rupert and Henry—they own the club. They were at school with me,' he explained.

'Hello, dear girl,' Rupert said. 'Delighted to meet you.'

'*Enchanté,*' Henry said, and kissed her hand.

'And this is Seraphina and Talia.'

Rupert and Henry's girlfriends? she wondered. They were incredibly elegant—reminding her of Audrey Hepburn on a really stellar day—and she felt totally out of place.

'Oh, I love your shoes,' one of them said.

'And your nail polish. Such a gorgeous colour.'

They both smiled at her—and then suddenly everything was all right. She'd been worrying about nothing.

She learned that Seraphina and Talia were both Rupert's sisters, and that Rupert and Henry were life partners as well as business partners.

'Marco bailed them out last year when the club was about to go into receivership. He won't let them pay him back until they're totally on their feet again. He's really one of the good guys,' Seraphina confided.

'He certainly is,' Rupert said, clearly overhearing the last bit. 'We used to call him El Princípe at school—The Prince.' He smiled. 'Though when he met my sisters and everyone else's we changed that to El Princípe Azul— Prince Charming.' He grinned. 'He was a hero to the rest of us, though—he stopped one guy bullying one of the little ones, even though he was four years older than Marco. Nobody's quite sure exactly what he did or said, but we know it involved a sword.'

Becca blinked. 'A sword?'

'And the school needed to buy a new mattress,' Henry added.

'You're telling me Marco killed someone?' she asked in a shocked whisper.

'Not quite, dear girl—wrong fluids. The guy wet himself to the point where the mattress was ruined.' Rupert smiled. 'Mind you, he never bullied anyone again after that.'

'Did he get into trouble?'

'Marco?' Henry grimaced. 'Um, yes—you can't exactly go round threatening people with swords, even if you *are* being a hero. The head confiscated his sword and banned him from fencing practice for the rest of the term—but we all knew the teachers were on his side about it.'

'Interestingly,' Rupert added, 'the bully left at the end of term and never came back.'

Becca wasn't surprised that Marco had helped a bullied child. It was totally who he was: protective and kind-hearted.

'You do know he's a serious fencer—that he's an international champion?' Henry asked.

Becca looked at Marco. 'I had no idea. You never said.'

Marco rolled his eyes. 'Honestly, it's not that big a deal.'

'A gold medallist, no less.' Rupert described a huge circle on his chest. 'Only our Marco would say it's no big deal. And you know when celebs open things by cutting ribbons? Well, El Princípe here does it with a sword.'

'Sabre,' Marco corrected dryly.

'It's still awesome—and he wears a dress uniform and looks…' Rupert fanned himself and grinned. 'Well. Such a shame you only like women, El Princípe Azul.'

''Fraid so.' Marco grinned back.

Becca smiled. 'Hey, Rupert, do you know what his surgeon called him at the clinic?'

Marco groaned. 'If you tell them that, Becca, they'll never let me live it down.'

'Too late, dear boy,' Rupert said. 'You have to tell us now, Becca, or we'll come and criticise your curtains.'

She couldn't help laughing; she liked Marco's friends immensely. 'I'm sure you'd never be so mean.'

'Come on, what did the surgeon call him, Becca?' Rupert asked, wagging his finger at her. 'Tell us. Tell us now.'

She paused for maximum effect. 'Zorro.'

Henry hooted in delight. 'How *perfect*. Wait a second.' He disappeared, and came back with a domino mask. 'Come on, dear boy, put it on.'

Marco gave him a pained look, but did so.

'Doesn't he look perfect? El Princípe, the freedom fighter—Zorro.' Henry looked pleased with himself.

Rupert looked at Marco. 'Hmm. Does the surgeon know about the medal, I wonder?'

'No—and you're not going to say anything to him, are you, Becca?' Marco said.

Becca just smiled. 'Tell me more, Henry.'

'Ferdy, now, he was the serious one who was top of the class at everything, but Marco here was the cool guy—the one who managed to make his uniform non-regulation, and he played lead guitar in a band,' Henry said.

That didn't surprise Becca in the slightest.

'Everyone's sister fell in love with him,' Rupert said, with a stern look at his own sisters, 'and he had hordes of girls trying to sneak into school to see him.'

'He's good at everything he does,' Henry said. 'If he wasn't such a nice guy, you'd have to hate him for it.'

'Oh, enough.' Marco flapped a dismissive hand. 'I'm going to get drinks. What's everyone having? Rupert, Henry, look after my girl,' he said, once he'd taken the list of what everyone wanted to drink.

Becca found herself surprisingly happy to be left with his friends. They weren't being nice to her for Marco's sake; they were being nice because they *were* nice.

'I haven't seen him smile like that for a long

time,' Rupert said. 'You've made a difference to him, Becca.'

She gave him a rueful smile. 'We don't come from the same world. I'm under no illusions here.'

'It doesn't matter where you come from,' Henry said, 'it's who you are that matters, how you treat other people. Marco believes that, too.'

Becca thought, *If only that could be true.* But her past was always going to get in the way. The only thing she could do was to make the most of now, store up the memories for the rest of her life.

'So we're dancing the tango tonight?' Marco asked when he returned with the drinks.

'You can't do it with one arm, Marco,' Rupert said.

'Yes, I can.'

Rupert rolled his eyes. 'Not if Becca hasn't done it before—unless you take the girl's part and let her lead, that is.'

Marco just grinned. 'Yeah, right. That's *so* going to happen.'

'Can I show you the steps, Becca?' Rupert asked.

She looked at Marco, who sighed. 'Rupert teaches this stuff for a living, so I guess he'll do a better job than I would.'

Rupert laughed. 'I should jolly well hope so.

Especially as right now you only have one arm! Come on, Becca, darling. Now, the tango is all about stalking. See how El Príncipe here is looking daggers at me right now? That's how a man's meant to look in the tango. And here we go. Slow-slow, quick-quick.' He talked her through the basic steps. 'And at the end, when you turn round, you stamp your feet—it's great when someone has spent all day annoying you and you can stomp about like this.'

She laughed. 'You think Marco spends all day annoying me?'

'Dear girl, he's a soldier and he orders people about. Of *course* he's annoying.'

And to think she'd been worried about coming here tonight. Marco had been right, after all—she was enjoying this, had relaxed, and was really having fun.

'And there's a lovely little move where you snap your head to the side—oh, but wait, the sling.' Rupert grimaced. 'It might not be kind to him. I don't want to hurt him.'

'Perhaps we'll leave that one for now,' she said.

'OK. But you can do the corner. Marco, no promenades, OK?' Rupert instructed.

Marco just rolled his eyes.

'Let's go through it again, dear girl. Marvellous. Now he can dance with you holding you only with his right hand.' He looked thought-ful. 'But the tango is special. We're not ready to dance that yet. We'll warm everyone up with some salsa first.'

Marco took off the domino mask and put it in his pocket.

'You have to wear it for the tango,' Henry said. 'I ought to see if I can find you a cape.'

'Great idea. Then we can make him do the Paso and wave the cape about,' Rupert agreed.

'Oh, please.' Marco rolled his eyes. 'Next thing you'll have me waving a sword about.'

'Now, there's an idea,' Rupert said with a grin.

'Becca, tell them I'm unbalanced with my arm like this,' Marco pleaded.

'Unbalanced, hmm?' Henry made a mocking circle with his forefinger on his temple.

Becca couldn't help laughing.

'I give up,' Marco said, and kissed her.

Becca was having a great time. Marco taught her the basic salsa steps, and she even recog-nised the music—*Living la Vida Loca* and *L'Americano*.

'Now, Rupert would tell you that the salsa is a party dance. Obviously if I had both arms working properly I could teach you different steps and the arm movements, but…' He gri-maced. 'Not tonight.'

She smiled. 'I'm glad you realise that will have to wait, bec—'

'Because it's not light work for my hand,' he cut in, using his good hand to make the sign of someone talking too much at her. 'Yeah, yeah. Heard it a thousand times.'

'Ah, so he's finally listening,' she teased back.

She was so glad he'd brought her here. This wasn't her usual kind of scene, but she enjoyed it, and nobody commented or tried to push her into having alcohol when she asked for sparkling water. She liked his friends, too; they seemed warm and genuine and really cared about him. And they were interested in her job, too; although when one of the girls asked for her advice about RSI Marco cut in gently, 'Hey, guys, she's off duty.'

'I don't mind. Call me at work,' Becca said, 'and I'll sort it out for you.'

They were taking a break from dancing when a woman sashayed over to them. She looked familiar, though Becca couldn't quite place her.

'Darling, how lovely to see you,' she said to Marco, and draped herself over him.

'Anastasia.' Marco was polite but seemed distant.

Anastasia kept glancing at Becca, but didn't

ask to be introduced and pretty much ignored her, concentrating all her energies on Marco.

That was when the penny dropped. Anastasia must have dated Marco at some time in the past. Becca was about to make an excuse that she needed the toilet, but Marco's fingers tightened round hers, as if he'd guessed that she was desperate to go and was asking her to stay.

Eventually Anastasia gave up trying to persuade Marco to dance with her, and left in a bit of a huff.

'Sorry about that,' Marco said. 'I didn't know she was going to be here tonight.'

'Is she an ex?' Becca asked softly.

He nodded. 'It was over months ago, but she wasn't too happy when I ended it.'

Becca knew how that felt—and she also knew she'd feel that way again.

'Becca—don't overthink this,' Marco said. 'I liked her when we dated, but there wasn't a real spark between us. It's not like how…'

She caught her breath—was he going to tell her how he felt about her?

Did he feel the same way about her as she did about him?

'Not like how things are between us,' he said softly. 'You're so different from the other women in my life.'

He could say that again, she thought wryly.

'There's something about you,' he said, 'something pure and innocent.'

Oh, help. He couldn't be more wrong.

'That's what drew me to you in South Africa, I think,' he said. 'You're not tarnished by life.'

Yes, she was. She'd been in rehab at sixteen. She'd seen the darkest sides of life. She'd watched people pour their lives away.

'I admire you,' he said, his eyes dark with sincerity. 'Really I do.'

How would Marco react if he knew the truth about her—if he knew that every day she had to remind herself to breathe and never, ever let her life spiral back to where it had been? He wouldn't admire her then. Nobody in their right mind would admire someone who'd skipped school in favour of vodka.

Maybe she should break it off now, before he could find out the truth about her and she saw his feelings change and crumble into dust.

And yet they'd agreed this was happy-for-now. They both knew their fling would have to end when he healed enough to go back to his royal duties. Was it so wrong of her to want to cherish these last few days together, to eke out every precious moment?

'Becca?' he asked softly. 'What's wrong?'

She was saved from having to answer when Henry came over and patted them both on the shoulder. 'It's time to tango. You need to wear your mask.'

Marco rolled his eyes but put the domino on.

When the music began, they went onto the dance floor.

'It's not the same with only one arm, but one day I'll dance with you properly,' Marco promised. 'For now, I'm afraid this will have to do.'

The music was incredibly sensual. Becca found herself picking up the beat easily after Rupert's earlier tutorial, especially as Marco guided her with his good arm and used his body to make her move the right way. He talked her through the steps: slow-slow, quick-quick, swaying along.

Then a spin. 'Quick-quick, turn; quick-quick, stamp—and we do it again,' he said.

Then they found themselves in the corner of the dance floor. Marco leaned over her and drew his hand into the small of her back, making her arch backwards. For a moment Becca's heart skipped a beat and she thought he was going to kiss her. But then he pulled back, guiding her with his good hand to lean over him, before repeating the move so that he was leaning over her and his lips were just millimetres from hers.

It took her breath away and the mask made

everything ten times worse, because it made him look like a movie star. Sexy as hell.

He danced her round the corner and along the next side of the room, keeping her close and his thighs thrust between hers.

'Oh, my God, Marco—I had no idea you could dance like this,' she said.

'I love the tango,' he told her. 'It's the same stance as boxing—but I'm more of a lover than a fighter.'

He was both, she thought. A lover and a fighter—for freedom and truth and decency.

And she loved every single bit of him.

She was shocked by how hot the dance made her feel—how much she wanted him. And it decided her: no, she wouldn't tell him about her past. She'd take these sweet, stolen moments as they were and not spoil them.

When the dance ended, he kissed her lingeringly.

'Marco—can we go home?' she asked.

He gave her a slow, sensual smile, as if he knew what she was really asking. 'Great idea. Let's go home.'

CHAPTER NINE

MARCO AND BECCA said a quiet goodbye to Henry and Rupert, then left the club wrapped in each other's arms. But the second they stepped outside the front door flashes started popping in their faces.

On instinct, Becca covered her face. This was just like the press pack outside the clinic when the news of Marco's injury broke. Except this time they appeared to be focused on him.

And on her.

Panic flooded through her. She prayed they hadn't caught a picture of her face. If they found out who she was they'd reveal her past to the world and, worst of all, to Marco. The man she'd lied to.

She had to get out of here.

Now.

Just as she was about to run, Marco clamped her to his side. 'Keep your head down and don't worry—just walk. I'll protect you.'

No, you can't protect me, she thought. *Nobody can protect me. Not now.*

Marco's bodyguard—who'd been so discreet that she hadn't even noticed him at the club—materialised on the other side and cleared a path to the car.

The noise levels were unbelievable. People were all talking and yelling at once, and she could barely make out the words; it was just a babble of noise. Flashbulbs were still going off, lighting up every step they took. What? Were they waiting for her to trip and fall over? For her skirt to fly up and show her knickers? They were like a crowd of teenage bullies, going on and on and on, and never shutting up. Pushing and pushing and pushing.

'Who's the girl, Marco?'

'Who's your lady friend?'

'Are you going to leave us a glass slipper, Cinderella?'

And the comments were interspersed with mocking catcalls and whistles, no doubt designed to make her look them in the eye so they could get a clear picture of her face.

'Ignore them. They're simply trying to get a reaction,' Marco said.

Just like playground bullies, she thought.

Except Marco wasn't going to be able to protect her as he'd protected the little boy at school by facing the bully down, because you couldn't face down the press. They'd find their story and twist it and twist it until they got their sensational headlines and their sales, not caring whose lives they wrecked in the process.

They just about made it to the car.

'Take me home,' she begged as she closed the car door on the rabble outside. 'Please take me home.'

'Rafa, back to Regent's Park, please,' Marco said.

'No, I want to go to *my* home,' Becca said, close to tears. 'They'll follow us to your place— if I go back to mine I can disappear and they won't find me. They don't know who I am so it'll all blow over.'

He took her hand. 'Becca, even if Rafa breaks a few speed limits, it won't make a difference. Some of the paps have motorbikes, so they will be able to keep up with us. And do you really want to be doorstepped at your place?'

She thought of how the paparazzi had been at the clinic, blocking the whole street to get a picture or a quote about one of their celebrity patients. That would be unthinkable in her quiet little street.

'At least at my home you'll be protected. You won't be out there on your own.'

She felt sick. Maybe she ought to tell him the

truth about her past, right here and now—but she just couldn't face seeing the disgust in his eyes if he knew what she was and what she'd done.

She hadn't cried since the day she'd found out Marco had abandoned her without a word in South Africa. She'd thought she'd cried out all her tears then—but now she found herself sobbing, unable to stop.

Marco hated feeling so useless. There was nothing he could say or do to make this right for her. He knew she'd seen the paps in action before, given that the Harley Street clinic where she worked treated celebrities, but nothing could prepare you for actually having it happen to *you*. He'd been used to it all his life, but he knew it must be overwhelming to someone who wasn't used to living in the public eye.

When they got back to Regent's Park, he made her a mug of hot milk and shooed Maria away. 'No, of course I haven't done anything to make her cry. It's shock because the press followed us. Don't worry, I'll look after her.'

Becca didn't drink the milk. All she did was cry silently.

'Talk to me, Becca,' he begged, seriously worried. 'You're blowing this out of proportion. Once they work out who the mystery girl is they'll have their story. They'll run on for a bit about the prince and the physio, and then it'll die down. There might be a couple of headlines—*Who's that girl?* or something like that—and then they'll find someone else to annoy.'

She shook her head and just looked at him in mute appeal.

He didn't understand why she was reacting this badly. What did she have to worry about? It didn't matter that she wasn't a socialite.

'Come on, let's go to bed,' he said. 'And, no, this isn't me trying to take advantage of you. It's me saying I want to hold you and make you feel safe until you fall asleep.'

To his horror, more tears streamed down her face.

'Becca, talk to me. What's wrong?'

She shook her head, clearly unable to get the words out.

'If I didn't have a busted arm, I'd carry you,' he said.

She looked horror-stricken at that, no doubt worried that he'd hurt himself.

He brushed his mouth lightly against hers. 'Come on, let's go to bed. Everything will be fine in the morning.'

He lay there with her curled against him. He knew she was still crying because he could feel the warmth and wetness of her tears against his skin, but he didn't know how to fix this, what to do or say. He just held her and hoped that he was right about the press and all would be fine in the morning.

All the same, he slept badly. Becca was clearly exhausted as he could hear her breathing, slow and deep; she wasn't faking sleep.

Unable to settle, he got up early, without waking her, and checked the news sites on the internet.

As he'd expected, there were a few *Who's that girl?* headlines.

But then he hit 'refresh' and saw the headlines of the story change.

My Nights of Shame with Prince's Lover...
What?

Marco flicked through the reports. They seemed to be focused on a guy called Barney, telling how Becca had been drunk out of her mind on vodka. According to him, she'd taken tablets to get high, then spent a sordid night with him.

No, this had to be some kind of mistake. Becca wasn't like that. She wasn't a wild child. The girl he'd met in South Africa had been sweet and shy. She'd been a virgin, for pity's sake. You couldn't fake that...could you?

And Marco knew for a fact that Becca didn't drink. He'd offered her champagne and cocktails and Pimm's, here on the roof garden, and she'd told him straight that she didn't drink. She'd drunk only mineral water last night at the club.

Then again, this could explain why she was teetotal. Because she'd had problems with drink before, now she couldn't trust herself with so much as a single sip of alcohol.

More news reports were coming through, all saying the same. Some had different levels of detail, but all of them said she'd been a wild child as a teen.

Why hadn't she told him?

Did she really think he would judge her for something that had happened years ago, when she was still little more than a child? Did she really think that he hadn't made some stupid mistakes himself?

He scanned another page and a fact leapt out at him.

Barney was in his late forties.

And if this had happened when Becca was sixteen, ten years ago…

What the hell had a man in his late thirties been doing with a teenager less than half his age?

Something about this wasn't right. Had the guy been grooming her? Had he been the one who'd given her the drink and the drugs?

Right at that second Marco wanted to hunt this Barney down. He wanted to pin the guy to the wall, with the tip of his sword at the scumbag's jugular vein, and demand some real answers.

And he was furious for himself for not protecting Becca. Why had he been so stupid and pushed her into going out for a night of fun at Mardi's when she'd been reluctant to go in the first place?

Henry and Rupert were loyal to him, he knew, and would have been more likely to create a diversion for the press to keep their attention off him rather than rat him out. But there had been someone else at the club who'd had an axe to grind, especially given that he hadn't gone there alone. He was pretty sure he knew who'd tipped the press off. There was nothing he could do about it now it had happened, but he could make Anastasia apologise to Becca and then warn everyone that he knew what she'd done, so they knew Anastasia couldn't be trusted and they'd need to be careful what they said and did around her in future.

He felt as if he'd been sucked into the middle of a seething cauldron of guilt, anger, and despair. He was guilty and angry with himself that he hadn't been able to protect Becca from all this spite and that she'd been hurt; he was angry with Becca that she'd kept something so huge from him; and he was despairing because he realised now that he'd been working towards the idea that his family might accept her as his life partner, but he knew all this mess would close the conservative royal circles to her. Anyone involved with the monarchy had to be totally squeaky clean. And even though Becca had been very young at the time it had happened—and he was damn sure she hadn't been the instigator of the drink, drugs and sex stuff—the mud was still going to stick.

He heard the door to the library close and looked up. Becca was standing there, fully dressed, looking pale and drawn and incredibly nervous.

Becca could see that Marco was reading something on the internet. If her phone hadn't been out of charge she would have checked the news herself. But she had a nasty feeling that the truth was out now. All of it. In every deeply shameful detail.

She couldn't tell from his expression how he felt about it. He'd said last night that he admired her. Now, would he despise her?

'Are you all right?' he asked.

She nodded, and swallowed hard. 'It's in the papers, isn't it? Everything?'

'Yes.'

The story must have travelled round the whole world before breakfast. And now everyone knew just how bad her past had been.

'Why didn't you tell me?' he asked.

'I couldn't—I was…' The words stuck in her throat. 'I was ashamed,' she whispered. 'So ashamed.'

Just as she could see now that he was ashamed of his relationship with her—and she couldn't blame him for it. After all, she'd just dragged his name into the mud along with hers.

'You should have told me,' he said.

Becca knew she was being unfair, taking out her shock and fear on him, but she couldn't help the anger bubbling over. 'Why? So you could judge me and find me wanting?'

'No. I'd never do that.' He stared at her. 'But I'm hurt that you didn't trust me. That you didn't feel you could tell me the truth.'

'It wouldn't have changed anything, would it? You can't change the past. I was a drunk and I went to rehab. Telling you wouldn't make me *not* have been a drunk. And I'm not a drunk any more. So what was the point of rehashing the past and telling you?'

'Because at least then I would've heard it from you. I wouldn't have had to find out from some spiteful, scurrilous article.'

That was true. But right now she couldn't think straight. The fear and the misery were uppermost. 'What's the point?' she asked. 'This thing between us—it's always been a fraud. Right from the start, in South Africa, when you lied about who you were. And this time round we couldn't even conduct a relationship in the open—it had to be kept a secret.'

'That's not fair,' Marco said. 'I wasn't the only one who wanted to keep it quiet. It suited you, too.'

Because she'd been an idiot and tried to hide from the truth. She should have known better.

'And,' he said, 'I might point out that I took you to meet my friends.'

She scoffed. 'We didn't even go to that club together. You went first, and I followed.'

'Because it was easier that way.'

'Easier for *you*. Do you have any idea how it felt, having to walk into a room on my own where you knew loads of people and I knew nobody?' Her eyes met his. 'You've lived such a privileged, pampered life—you have absolutely no idea what the real world's like.'

'Says the woman who works in a clinic catering to the rich and pampered,' he snapped back.

She flinched. 'We do a lot of charity work at 200 Harley Street. It isn't all facelifts and cosmetic procedures.'

'No?'

'No, it damn well isn't! You should know—they treated *you*. And I might not even have a career there any more.'

The one thing that had been certain in her life and now it wasn't. Fear of what was going to happen next made her bones feel as if they'd turned to liquid.

'Now all my past's been dragged up people aren't going to want me to treat them. I might even be struck off the register for unprofessional behaviour. It's all right for someone like you—you've got a family behind you, people who have your back. The only person I can really rely on is me—and I'm not going to be able to save myself from this.'

She shook her head.

'I can't stay here any more.' Not being so close to him, and knowing that he could never be hers any more. It was too much for her. She wanted out.

'You can't go. The paps are knee-deep outside,' he said wearily.

Not *Don't go because I love you and I want you to stay,* she noticed. He was worried about his *reputation*, not her. How had it come to this? How had all the love just leaked away overnight to leave them with nothing?

'I'll take my chances with them.' She lifted

her chin. 'You know as well as I do it could never have worked out between us. We would never have got together in a million years. A prince can't date an addict—even a reformed one. But this time, Marco, this time *I* get to be the one to walk away.' Even though walking out on him was going to be like ripping her heart out.

How stupid she'd been to let herself fall in love with him all over again. With a man she knew was out of her reach, a man she could never have. They'd been living in a bubble, and now it was time to face the truth. It was over.

'Don't bother sending my stuff after me,' she said. 'Just throw it away. I don't want it any more.' Not when everything would be soaked in memories of him.

As Becca walked out, Marco was too shocked to stop her or follow her.

She clearly wasn't going to listen to his side of things.

Just when he'd been sure that he'd found someone who actually loved him for himself—someone who'd loved him before she even knew that he was a prince—he realised that he hadn't.

If she'd really loved him then she would have known she could tell him anything and it wouldn't matter.

The fact that she'd kept such a dark secret from him just proved that she didn't trust him—and if she didn't trust him, then how could he trust her?

So maybe she was right and it was better this way.

Maybe he should just let her go.

Because you couldn't give someone a royal order to love you. You couldn't order them to feel something they didn't feel.

And she was right, too, about them never getting together in a million years—they came from such different places. This was a reality check. The bubble had burst.

The only thing was, he didn't want it to be over.

And he didn't see how it could be anything *but* over.

Angry, hurt and just a tiny bit bitter, Marco sat at the piano and, one-handed, played all the saddest music he knew—music of pain and heartbreak and misery. And even then it couldn't express how he felt because he couldn't add in the bass, the deep notes of despair.

Becca left everything behind in the house at Regent's Park except her handbag.

Marco hadn't come after her. How stupid she'd been to hope that he'd care enough to follow her, that he'd ask her not to go and tell her they could work something out. The fact that he hadn't just proved that she'd just been a diversion for a bored prince while he waited for his hand to heal.

The press were waiting outside for her.

This time she wasn't going to let them make her cry. Or run. They could all go to hell, as far as she was concerned. Because she really didn't care any more. She didn't care about anything. Because she didn't have a heart left to care.

She just ignored the cameras flashing and the questions being yelled at her and strode through the park until she got to the Tube station. She was relieved that she already had a season ticket and didn't have to worry about buying a ticket. She lost some of the press pack in the morning rush hour as she went through the ticket barrier, then quickened her pace and took the left-hand side of the escalator so she could rush down in the middle of a pack of commuters instead of being trapped in one place. As she was halfway down the escalators, she felt the cool breeze signalling that a train was coming in and quickened her pace again. It didn't matter that the train was going in the wrong direction; she could sort that out later. She heard the station announcement telling passengers to mind the doors, and managed to squeeze on to the train.

Thank God none of the press pack was quick enough to follow her. No doubt they'd all been barged out of the way by irritated commuters.

Becca stayed on the train until it stopped at Embankment. Then she joined the throng of commuters, changed over to the Circle line, and caught the Tube through to Paddington. Hopefully the press wouldn't have managed to dig up her address yet.

She kept her head down as she left the train, but there was no sign of waiting paparazzi. Relieved, she headed for her flat and locked the door behind her.

Safe at last.

But just what did she do now?

Technically, she was still working one to one with Marco, so her caseload at the clinic was still being covered and she didn't have to worry about missing any appointments. But she knew that the rest of the staff would have seen the news. She couldn't just pretend that nothing had happened; she had to face it.

Just…not quite yet.

It was still early, officially before the start of the main day at the clinic, so with any luck she'd get the answering machine instead of the receptionist and could leave a message to buy herself a little more time and work out what to say. How to explain. How to apologise.

To her relief, the answering machine kicked in. 'Sorry, it's Becca,' she said. 'I'm not feeling well. I'm not working today. I'll keep you posted. Sorry.' Aware that she was gabbling, and not wanting to risk that someone would hear the message as she was speaking and pick up the phone, she hung up.

A few moments later the doorbell rang. Marco? Her heart leapt at the thought.

She picked up the Entryphone. 'Yes?'

'Becca Anderson?'

It was a voice she didn't recognise—and there was the kind of hubbub in the background that told her some of the journalists had managed to get hold of the electoral roll and found her details on it. Of course it wouldn't be Marco. He didn't even know where she lived.

She didn't answer the journalist, and hung up without pressing the button to let anyone in.

The doorbell rang again and again, but she ignored it.

No doubt now they were after her side of the story, to see if they could fill in any juicy details that Barney had left out.

Well, tough. They weren't going to get it. She had nothing to tell them.

Becca spent the next three days holed up in her apartment, not answering the phone or the door or emails, and keeping her mobile phone turned off most of the time. When she did turn it on, she deleted all messages from Marco without reading them and just ignored the ones from work. She still couldn't face talking to anyone. Not even Lexi, who'd left several messages before Becca's answering machine was filled to the max, and then texted her saying she was there whenever Becca needed to talk.

What should she do now?

The first thing would be to resign. The stories about her were just too awful; if she stayed, her reputation would drag down the clinic. Patients wouldn't want to be treated by someone like her. But leaving the clinic meant she'd have to give up her flat, too. She wouldn't be able to afford it without a job. And where was she going to find another job? She still wasn't sure if she'd be struck off the register for unprofessional conduct, but even if she wasn't she could hardly ask for a reference. Without a reference she'd be unemployable. All her dreams, all her future—gone.

And the worst bit was how much she missed Marco. Last time round she'd been a naïve teenager. This time round she was a strong, independent woman. She'd made exactly the same mistake. And, this time it hurt more. Missing him was a physical ache. The rest of her life stretched out in front of her, and there was nothing left to fill it. Just a black hole where she wished Marco could be.

And all the time the press remained camped outside the block of flats. In the end, she disconnected the Entryphone because she was tired of the constant calling.

When Becca finally managed to slip out of the back entrance to her block of flats, without the paparazzi following her, she went straight to Harley Street.

'Is Ethan in?' she asked Helen, the receptionist on duty.

'Yes, he's in his office,' Helen said. 'Are you all right, Becca?'

No, she wasn't all right, and she didn't think anything would ever be all right again. She gave the receptionist a sad little smile in answer, went to Ethan's office and rapped on the open door.

He looked up from his desk. 'Becca, you look like crap,' he said bluntly.

'I'm sorry I let you down and went off sick,' Becca said. 'I wasn't really sick. I just couldn't…'

'It's OK. I understand,' he soothed her.

She took a deep breath. 'I'll resign.'

'You most certainly will not,' Ethan said. 'You're an excellent hand therapist and we don't want to lose you. Your resignation is not accepted.'

'But all the stuff in the papers...'

'I don't care—well, I do,' he said, 'because I hate to think that you had such a rough time growing up, and I'd like to scoop out that Barney's heart with a rusty blunt scalpel.' He smiled at her. 'And, believe you me, I'd have to fight for my place at the front of the queue to do that.'

She stared at him, not quite believing this.

'Look, I know what it's like to have a parent who drinks.'

She nodded. She'd heard the rumours, even though it had all happened years ago—which was also why she knew the stories about her would run and run and run.

'It's not pleasant. And look at you now—you've pulled yourself out of that world. It all happened years ago, and it's totally not relevant to what you do now.'

'But won't the patients—well—prefer not to be treated by someone like me?' Becca asked.

'Are you kidding? Mrs van der Zee has been ringing every day to see if you're back yet, and she's not the only one—they're all worried about you.'

Becca felt the tears well up and blinked them back.

'You belong here,' Ethan said, 'and we've got your back, Becca. You're one of us.'

She really belonged?

Really, *really?*

She couldn't trust herself to speak, at first, but eventually she managed a broken 'Thank you.'

'Anyway, where the hell is Zorro? Why hasn't he protected you from the monsters in the press?' Ethan demanded.

'We— It's over,' she said in a whisper.

Ethan said something very pithy about what Marco was lacking.

'That's not quite fair, Ethan. I was the one who walked out on him.'

'But he should've come to get you back. He's an idiot and he doesn't deserve you.' Ethan narrowed his eyes. 'And I told him not to flirt with my staff. I thought he'd understand that meant anything further than flirting was way off limits.'

Becca couldn't say anything to that.

'Right. Lexi will help deal with the press— we'll get this sorted and minimise the damage. And we want you back to work, so go and scrub your face. When did you last eat?'

'I can't remember,' she admitted. Since the story had broken, she hadn't felt like eating.

'Well, you can't live on fresh air. Go down to the buffet and grab some breakfast—I don't want you fainting on anyone—and then get in that white coat and back in your office, OK?'

'OK.' It was so, so much more than she'd hoped for. So much more than she thought she deserved. 'Thank you.'

Funnily enough, eating breakfast did make her feel better. And so did the fact that every single member of the clinic dropped in to see her, give her a hug, and say that they were on her side.

'You idiot. Why didn't you tell me?' Lexi hugged her. 'You know what I do for a living. You know I could've spun this for you and saved you from all the nonsense.'

Becca was too close to tears to answer.

Lexi hugged her again. 'And we're friends, right?'

Friends. This time, a tear trickled down her cheek. 'I think so,' she whispered.

'I know so,' Lexi said. 'Even though you always keep so much of yourself back.'

'I'm not used to having friends,' Becca said. 'When I was little…' She dragged in a breath. 'People got sick of my mum being late to pick me up from playdates. And they noticed that she smelled of drink. So they didn't encourage their kids to be my friend. I was always the child in the class who didn't get invited to any of the birthday parties.'

Lexi stroked her hair. 'That sucks.'

'It's how it was. It was my life.' She dragged in a breath. 'It wasn't so bad when I was a teen. You know how kids like to rebel against their parents—so my home life didn't stop them being friends with me. Or *trying* to be. Nobody ever taught me how to make friends. I wasn't very good at it.' She looked away. 'Then I started drinking. I wasn't nice to be around. I was an embarrassment to everyone.'

'The teen years are hard,' Lexi said softly. 'Harder still if you don't get support from your parents.'

Becca narrowed her eyes. 'That sounds personal.'

'It is. The way you look…' Lexi shook herself. 'Enough of that. But the important thing is not to stop believing in yourself. Look what you did. You were dragged into the kind of world a teenager should never be dragged into. And you got yourself out of it. You studied hard, and you got yourself a really good job. You're stronger than you think.'

'Right now I don't feel strong. I feel stupid.' Becca blinked away the tears. 'What was I thinking, having an affair with Marco? He's a prince. Of course the likes of him aren't for me.'

'Why not?'

Becca found herself telling Lexi the whole

messy story. How she'd fallen in love with 'Seb'
at the camp and he'd broken her heart. How
she'd met Marco again at the clinic and they
hadn't been able to stop themselves falling all
the way back in love. And now… 'He didn't
ask me to stay or say he'd help me fix things.'

'Did you give him the chance to ask you to
stay?' Lexi asked.

'Maybe not,' Becca admitted. She bit her lip.
'He was pretty angry because I hadn't told him
the truth.'

'Angry because you hadn't trusted him,
maybe,' Lexi said.

'That night, just before the press lay in wait
for us, he said he admired me. That I was sweet
and innocent and untarnished.' She closed her
eyes. 'Now he despises me.'

'Did he say that?'

'He didn't have to.'

'Does it not occur to you that there's a lot to
admire about you?' Lexi asked. 'Look at the
way you've overcome your past.'

'That's just PR spin,' Becca said.

'No. It's the truth. Look at yourself properly,
Becca. You've got so much to give. And Marco
has a point. What happened wasn't your fault.
You were a child. People were supposed to look
after you, not drag you down into the mire.'

'I could've said no.'

'When was the last time you had a drink?'

Becca thought about it. 'Before rehab.'

'Years ago. Exactly. You're strong, Becca. You're amazing. And that's what Marco would've seen if you'd trusted him with the truth. I don't know him that well, but what I do know is that he has integrity. Give the man a chance. Trust him—and then you can really move on from your past.'

'I think it's too late for that.' Becca shook her head. 'I'm totally unsuitable for him. His parents would never approve.'

'His parents,' Lexi said, 'are surprisingly down to earth. And they're very easy to work with in PR terms. You need to take that step forward, Becca. Trust yourself. And trust him. I know it's easier said than done, but think about it.' She hugged Becca again. 'I'll see you later, with my PR hat on, and we'll get a few things sorted. But, for now, just remember I'm here. As your friend.'

The lump in her throat was so huge Becca could hardly speak. 'I will,' she whispered.

Becca's first patient of the day was Mrs van der Zee.

'Are you sure you still want me to treat you?' Becca asked. 'After all the stuff in the press?'

'Which no doubt they exaggerated to sell more filthy copies.'

'Not that much,' Becca said. 'I was addicted to vodka and E.'

'You were sixteen, still a child, and it wasn't your fault,' Mrs van der Zee said. 'That man has a lot to answer for. I think every parent in the country wants to find that man and make quite sure he can never do anything like that again.'

Becca felt the tears well up again. She hadn't expected people to be so kind.

And it made it hurt even more that the one person she'd wanted to believe in her, root for her, had just abandoned her and left her to it.

Mrs van der Zee hugged her. 'It'll work out, love—don't you worry. And I think that prince of yours needs a good kick up the backside, war hero or no war hero.'

That earned her a watery smile. 'He's one of the good guys.'

'Well, he should be here protecting you and making the press go away,' Mrs van der Zee said. 'Now, shall we get started?'

Becca wouldn't answer a single one of Marco's calls, and either the clinic was protecting her or she'd totally gone to ground. All the curtains in her flat were drawn. The door hadn't been answered when he'd sent a discreet box of chocolates to apologise—because he knew damn well that the press would make a big deal of it if he sent a huge bouquet that she refused to accept. Being Becca, she *would* refuse to accept it.

The only reason that he hadn't gone to get her himself was because he knew that it would make the press speculation much, much stronger, and they'd make her life even harder. At times like this he really hated his background and wished that he was just an ordinary man who wouldn't be noticed going about his day-to-day business—that he could put things right without every movement being scrutinised in the public eye.

But the worst bit was the huge hole in his life now Becca wasn't here. He hated being without her. The future was just lonely and bleak, stretching out for eternity. Nothing but his duty to sustain him. And that would be his royal duty; he had to be honest and admit that the injury to his hand would make it next to impossible to go back to active service in the army. Anything less than full fitness would put his men in jeopardy, and he wasn't prepared to be that selfish.

Just his royal duty, and no Becca to help him through it.

Then again, if he had Becca in his life it meant he couldn't have his family. He couldn't bring disrepute on the monarchy and the mud would most definitely stick, even though Becca was clearly clean of drink and drugs now.

If he stayed as Prince Marco, he'd be without the love of his life.

If he became an ordinary man, he'd be without his family.

Why couldn't he have come from an ordinary family so none of this would matter? What was so wrong with wanting love *and* your family? Why couldn't you have both? There had to be a way. There just had to be.

And he couldn't sort it out in England. He needed to be back in Sirmontane and talking it over with the two people who could help him make it happen. He needed them to understand how he really felt. And maybe, just maybe, they could work it out.

Four hours later, Marco walked into his parents' drawing room in the castle.

'My son.' Elena, his mother, greeted him with a hug. 'You look absolutely terrible.'

He rolled his eyes. 'Thanks, Mamá.'

'I'm your mother. I'm not going to lie to you.' She hugged him again.

Alfonso, too, hugged Marco. 'Your mother has been worrying about you.'

'I'm healing.' He indicated his left hand. 'I get to do more this month.'

'Not just about your injury. We've read the papers,' Elena said.

And no doubt they thought the worst of Becca. 'She's not like the press paint her,' he said. 'She's not a wild child at all. She's brave and she's managed to overcome her past—she's worked hard and made a good career for herself. There's a lot to admire about her.'

'I agree, the press are spinning it,' Elena said, surprising him. 'She was vulnerable when it happened. Still a child. And it wasn't her fault that she was led into the darker edges of life.'

'I agree, too. And as for Barney, I'd horse-whip him myself,' Alfonso said.

The guy who'd groomed her. 'I'll kill him,' Marco said.

'No—and we don't want another incident like that one with the sword at school,' Alfonso said. 'You're not a hothead in the army. Don't be a hothead outside it. Think before you act. How many times have I told you that?'

'And how many times haven't I listened?' Marco asked wryly.

'You are who you are.' Elena smiled at him. 'So you knew Becca before you met her at the clinic?'

'I first met her in South Africa, at the children's aid camp.' Marco grimaced. 'Then Abuelo was taken to hospital. I went back for her when the doctors said he would pull through, but she'd already left South Africa. Vanished.'

'And you didn't tell her where you were going in the first place, did you?' Elena asked, rolling her eyes. 'Why are boys so hopeless when it comes to communicating?'

'That's why we get married, *cariña*,' Alfonso said, kissing her. 'So our wives can do it for us.'

She flapped a dismissive hand. 'This is about our son, not you.'

'Though Papá has a point,' Marco said dryly.

'Yes, I suppose he does.' She sighed. 'Sometimes, Marco, for a man who can be so bright, I wonder how you can be quite so stupid. Do you know that Becca is still involved with the rehab centre that helped her?'

'How do you know that?' he asked, surprised that his parents seemed to know a lot more about the situation than he did.

'We've been working with Lexi at the clinic,' Alfonso said.

'Becca's a volunteer at the rehab centre,' Elena explained. 'She talks to young girls like she was, girls who are addicted to drink and worse, and helps them find their way back to a happier life.'

The penny suddenly dropped. That was the 'commitment' Becca had been so vague about. And of course she wouldn't have been able to tell him about it, because then she would have had to explain why she helped there.

And now for the crunch issue. The one that could divide him from his family. But he needed it to be out in the open.

'Becca's the only woman I've ever really loved. The woman I want to spend the rest of my life with. I know it's all a mess, and lots of people are going to think she's totally unsuitable to be a princess. But I'm so miserable without her.' He bit his lip. 'I've been thinking about it. I'm prepared to give up being a prince, if that's what it takes to make her acceptable as my wife. But I don't want to lose my family. I don't want to have to choose between you. And that's why I came home. To talk to you. To see if there was a way I could still be your son but be with the woman I love.'

'My darling boy, you would *never* have to choose between us. We're your parents and we will always love you, no matter what you do and even when you make us worried sick. We want you to be happy,' Elena said. She tutted. 'Alfonso, I told you he was stupid. How could he think such a thing?' She cuffed Marco's good arm.

'So you would accept Becca,' he said carefully, 'as my wife?'

'We think she's a shining example of strength and grace, someone who's lived through hard times and come out the other side to help others who fall into the same traps,' Alfonso said. 'And other European princes have married women who are not of royal birth. This is the twenty-first century. There isn't the same issue over class that there was for my father, or my father's father.'

Hope flared in Marco's heart for the first time in days. 'With Becca at my side I'll be a better man. A better prince.'

'A better soldier?' Elena asked dryly.

He shook his head. 'I have to be honest. My hand will heal, but I might never regain the full range of movement or grip. I won't be able to do my job properly, and I won't put other people at risk just for the sake of my pride. I'm prepared to accept an honourable discharge, or just finish my tour of duty as a pen-pusher. And then that's it. I'm back in the fold and ready to begin my royal duties.'

Elena hugged him. 'For that alone I would gladly accept Becca. Because having her in your life will take you out of danger.'

'Small problem,' Marco said. 'She's not talking to me right now.'

'So you think she'll turn you down?'

'I'm going to eat humble pie,' Marco said. 'And I'm going to tell her how I really feel about her. And then, with luck, she'll agree to make me the happiest prince in the world.'

'Go, *niño*,' his father said, 'with our blessing.'

Elena coughed. 'We'll be going to London, too.'

Alfonso frowned. 'Why?'

'To meet our future daughter-in-law.'

'Mamá, much as I love you, I'm not having that conversation with Becca in front of you,' Marco said.

Elena laughed. 'Of course not. But I'm looking forward to meeting her. And you can tell her that, too—not in an intimidating way, but in a welcoming way.'

Marco smiled. 'That's a royal order I'd be very happy to carry out.'

'I'll call Carlos and have the plane sorted out,' Alfonso said. 'And you need to do your exercises and then rest your hand, *niño*.'

CHAPTER TEN

FIRST THING THE next morning, Rafa drove Marco to the back entrance of the Hunter Clinic, and Marco slipped inside.

The receptionist looked at him. 'Can I help you, Your Highness?'

Either she recognised him from his stay at the clinic, or she'd seen the newspapers. Given the slight coolness of her tone behind the politeness, he had a nasty feeling it was the latter. Of course everyone here would be protective of Becca.

'I was, ah, hoping to see Becca Anderson.' He indicated his strapped-up arm. 'I'm due a physiotherapy session.'

'I see. If you wouldn't mind waiting over there, Your Highness, I'll see if I can find her for you,' the receptionist said, gesturing to the waiting area.

Marco sat down on one of the plush white leather sofas. He ignored the glossy magazines on the low coffee table; right at that moment he couldn't concentrate on anything. He just needed to see Becca.

But would she agree to see him?

He looked up hopefully as he heard someone come down the corridor. Except the tall male figure wasn't the one he wanted to see.

Ethan Hunter looked grim. 'Shall we go to my office, Your Highness?'

Oh, hell. He wasn't here to have a fight. He was here to make things right.

'Sure,' he said, and followed the surgeon to his office.

Though he declined to have a seat.

'So what you do want, Your Highness?' Ethan asked.

Marco sighed inwardly. It wasn't just his relationship with Becca that he'd messed up; he'd crushed his burgeoning friendship with the spiky ex-army doctor, too. 'I need to see Becca,' he said.

'Uh-huh.' Ethan gave him a level stare. 'I told you not to flirt with my staff, but you completely ignored me. In fact, you did more than that. So, tell me, why the hell should we even let you back here?'

'Because I need to see Becca.'

'I don't give a damn who you are—prince or no prince, you hurt Becca, and that's not acceptable. We have a zero tolerance policy and no money or celebrity or royal status will ever change that.'

Marco knew he deserved every bit of the reprimand. 'I screwed up,' he said softly. 'But, hand on heart, Clavo, can you tell me you've never made a mistake? Can you tell me you've never hurt a woman? Someone you loved? Because everything around you got messed up and the right words wouldn't come out?'

Ethan said nothing, and Marco knew he'd hit home. Whatever Ethan Hunter had done probably wasn't quite in the same league as the way Marco had messed up, and it certainly hadn't been done on the stage of the world's media circus, but all the same Marco could tell that the surgeon knew what it was like to get it badly wrong.

'I need to see Becca,' he repeated. 'I need to apologise to her properly. I need to tell her that I love her and I don't give a damn about where she comes from or what she's done in the past— it's the present and the future that matters. Who she is now.'

Ethan didn't look convinced.

Marco drew in a breath. 'I know she doesn't have family to look out for her, and the people here at the clinic and the rehab centre are the nearest she has to a family. I'm glad you're all looking out for her—and I can assure you my intentions towards her are completely honourable.'

Ethan was silent for so long that Marco thought he'd blown it.

But then the surgeon nodded. 'Just so you know, if you do anything to upset her or hurt her, I'll come after you myself. Limp or no limp.'

'I'm not going to hurt her,' Marco said. 'I'm going to grovel. And I just hope she can find it in her to forgive me and give me a second—no, a third chance.'

'Three strikes and you're out, I'd say.'

Marco gave him a wry smile. 'I'd better make sure I get it right this time.'

'Yeah, you'd better. She's in her office,' Ethan said. 'I assume you know where that is?'

'I do. And thank you.'

When the surgeon had left, Marco went down the corridor to Becca's office and rapped on the door.

She looked up, as if to welcome in a patient, and her face went white. '*You*. What are you doing here?'

'I believe I have a physiotherapy appointment,' he said. 'Phase two.'

She shook her head. 'I'm not treating you any more.'

'I can understand why you'd rather not treat me,' he said carefully, 'and I'll accept your decision—but will you please listen to me before you make that decision?'

Her eyes narrowed. 'Like you listened to me?'

'Technically,' he said, 'you didn't give me the chance to listen to you. You blew up and stormed out. And, yes, I know I should've run straight after you and stopped you leaving. I was a fool. I let stuff get in the way.'

She said nothing, but at least she hadn't thrown him out.

'I don't care about your background, Becca. I don't care where you came from or what happened in your past,' he said. 'Well, I *do* care— I hate that you were treated so badly when you were a vulnerable teenager, by someone who should've looked after you instead of dragging you down—but what I mean is that the past doesn't matter. I love the girl you were when I first met you, and I love the woman you are now.'

'You love me?' she said. 'But nothing can come of it. You're a prince and I...' She blew out a breath. 'Well. The press labelled me a wild child.'

'Because they know only half the story. Something that someone fed them. By the time I've finished talking to them they're going to see you for exactly who you are,' he said. 'A brave, talented woman. Someone who's a real role model—someone who's come through adversity and built a decent life for herself. I'm proud of you.'

She curled her lip. 'You didn't seem proud the other day. You were angry.'

'I was, but not with you,' he said. 'I was angry with myself. I should've protected you better. And I should've seen for myself that you can fit into my world. You're good enough, Becca. More than good enough.'

'What made you see it differently?'

'Being without you. Because it was like a black hole. I saw my future without you, and it was so bleak and lonely and miserable.' He looked at her. 'My parents have been talking to Lexi. Nobody's broken any confidences—but they did tell me that you volunteer at a rehab clinic. And I'm guessing that's your way of paying back for the way you were helped.'

She frowned. 'Yes—but…' She looked confused, unable to take things in. 'Your parents?'

'They hold you in pretty high esteem,' he said. 'I guess what I'm saying is if you'll have me, and put up with the royal engagements and media circus that kind of have to go along with me, then…' He had nothing to lose, now. So he'd tell her just how he felt. 'Becca, you make me a better man. I feel complete when I'm with you. I know I've hurt you, more than once, and I'd like the chance to make that up to you. Will you marry me?'

'But—what about the drink and the drugs? I'm totally unsuitable for a prince's consort or what have you.'

He shrugged. 'Everyone makes mistakes. Sometimes they're helped to make those mistakes, dragged into it by someone else. It's in the past. You can't go back and change it. But you can learn from your mistakes, put them behind you—and you've gone one step further than that, because you're helping other people who've ended up in the same trap you were in. And they'll listen to you because they know you've been there and come out the other side so you understand what it's really like. It takes someone really special to do that, to help people like that. So will you marry me?'

She bit her lip. 'Marco, I can't give you an answer. Not while this is all hanging over me.'

'I hope you know that you have my family's backing. And the backing of everyone here. And I'd guess it's the same at the rehab place. You're not alone,' he said softly.

'I was alone for a long time,' she said, suddenly looking very young and vulnerable.

He held out his free arm. 'If telling me the

whole story will help you, I'll listen. And I won't judge,' he said softly.

Would telling him the whole story help her?

At least it would mean they had no more secrets. No more lies between them.

She stood up from her chair and walked round to his side of the desk. Let him hold her.

All these years of standing on her own two feet and now, for once, it felt good to have someone to lean on.

She dragged in a breath. 'My dad died when I was tiny. It was an accident. My mum didn't cope very well—she wanted someone who'd look after her and love her, the way he had. I had a lot of "uncles", but she never seemed to find the right one. And in the end she started drinking to help her forget how unhappy she was.' She looked at him. 'And I mean hard drinking. Half the time she forgot I was there, too. I learned to make a jam sandwich before I could even write my name.'

'Oh, Becca.'

She shrugged. 'Plenty of people have it as bad as that. They don't have much money; bread and jam's cheap, it fills you up and it doesn't need cooking.'

He stroked her hair. 'OK. I'm not judging.'

Though she could see in his eyes that he was angry on her behalf.

'It doesn't get better,' she said. 'But I understand why, now. My mum was lost. She couldn't find her way out. I guess she was needy—and it was too much for a new partner. Every time she met someone and I thought it was going all right, because she was going to have a baby and we'd be a family... Well, she found it hard to cope when the baby cried. Then she'd drink. Pick fights. Then her partner would get tired of her drinking and leave. And that would make her feel worse, and the only way she could feel better was to drink enough to make her forget.'

'Hard on you.'

'Not just me. I've got, what, four or five brothers and sisters. Half-brothers and sisters,' she amended. 'Not that I've seen any of them since they were two years old. Their dads got custody—well, what with my mum's drinking, it was probably better they lived with their dads than with us.'

'What about you? Didn't any of them try to take custody of you?'

She shrugged. 'I wasn't their child. They didn't want me.'

'But why didn't you get taken into care? Surely the authorities knew from the court cases that your mum was drinking and not looking after you. Didn't anyone speak up for you?'

'There wasn't anyone to speak up for me.' She shrugged. 'It was OK. I managed. I mean—it hurt that nobody ever invited me to birthday parties, but I understood why. The other mums didn't like my mum. She'd get drunk and try to flirt with every man in sight.' She sighed. 'We did OK until I was fifteen—and then she started seeing Barney.' She bit her lip. 'He started putting vodka in my lemonade. I didn't realise what was happening at first—you can't taste vodka, can't smell it. But it quickly got so I felt I needed something. He talked to me in the kitchen one night, and I must've said something because he gave me a drink. It made me feel better. So I had more. And I...I was horrible when I was drunk. I fell out with the few friends I did have, because of my drinking. And drinking more helped to blot out how miserable I was.'

Marco looked at her. 'You were *fifteen*. Too young to drink.'

'Too young to buy it for myself from a shop or a pub, and too young to drink in a public place,' she corrected. 'But it's harder to police what goes on behind closed doors. There were lots of underage kids at the rehab centre.'

'So he let you drink vodka. He encouraged you.'

'And then one night he kissed me.' She closed her eyes briefly, remembering how disgusting she'd found it. How he'd slobbered over her. How she'd wanted to scream herself sick when he'd put his hands under her clothes but she'd been too scared to make a noise, because Barney had told her to keep quiet or her mum would be upset.

But her mum had been upset anyway.

'My mum caught us, and he told her…' She dragged in a breath, still outraged by how easily Barney had lied, and how her mother had actually believed him. 'He said I came on to him. She accused me of trying to steal her boyfriend, and she threw me out.'

Marco stroked her hair. 'Where did you go?'

'I didn't have anywhere to go,' she said. 'I'd fallen out with everyone at school because of the drinking, so I couldn't ask to stay with anyone. I thought I was going to have to live on the streets. I was just walking round, trying to see a doorway where I could shelter for the night. But then Barney came after me. He said he'd look after me. That I could stay at his flat. And he had a spare room.' She bit her lip. 'I thought he felt guilty about what he'd done and was trying to be nice, helping me out. I thought he was going to soften my mum up a bit so she'd let me go back home and I'd stop crying round his flat. Except…'

She looked away.

'That wasn't quite what he had in mind. He said he had something for me, something that would make me feel better. And he gave me this tablet.'

'You took it?'

'I was drunk at the time. Of course I took it.' She swallowed hard. 'And then a couple of weeks later, when he'd given me more and more, he said I owed him for the drugs I'd taken. And the vodka. I didn't have any money. He said I could—I could pay him in kind. Give him my virginity. And…' Oh, this was so hard to say. 'He was going to film it,' she whispered. 'Make money from it. Sell it to people who wanted to watch.'

Marco held her close. 'Oh, my Becca. I want to kill him. Very, very slowly. The traditional death from a thousand cuts.'

'He didn't actually do it,' she said. 'Because I told him I couldn't do it, it was the wrong time of the month. And he said as soon as—as soon as I was clean, he'd do it.'

Marco held her tighter.

'But I went to school that day,' she said. 'I'd been skipping lessons. I didn't care about school any more. But for some reason I felt I had to go in that day. We had a Personal Development class. There was a woman there from the rehab centre, giving us all a talk about drugs. After the talk I asked to leave the classroom to go to the loo, but I followed her out to her car, and I asked her to help me get into rehab—to help me get away from Barney. And she told the school I was going with her, and she took me to the rehab centre. They helped me get off the vodka and the drugs.'

'What about Barney? *Please* tell me she skewered Barney. That he was put in prison for what he did.'

She shook her head. 'He said I was lying. It was my word against his. He said I'd tried it on with him and he'd turned me down because I'd only just turned sixteen, and he said I was just trying to get my own back by smearing his good name.'

'How could the police let him get away with it?'

'I had no evidence. It was all circumstantial. Like I said, it was my word against his.'

'But surely your mum stood up for you and told them what he did?'

'She was still angry with me. She said nothing.'

'Oh, Becca.'

'I never lived with her again,' Becca said.

'The rehab centre found me a place to live, and got me made a ward of the court so I couldn't be taken anywhere without their permission. Barney couldn't come and get me. And I was determined I'd prove their faith in me, that I'd make something of myself. I passed my exams—I crammed everything at the last minute and my grades weren't brilliant, because I'd had a year of skipping classes and being drunk, but I passed enough to go on to sixth form. I did better with my A levels, earned a place at university. The rest you know.'

'You truly are amazing,' Marco said. 'And I'm so proud of you.'

She blinked back the tears. 'I'm *not* going to cry.'

'Only happy tears, from now on,' he said. He stroked her face. 'Did you make it up with your mother?'

'Not really. After she split up with Barney she drank even more. She ended up with oesophageal varices. One day, she bled out. It was just before my A levels.' She swallowed hard. 'The emergency department called her neighbour, who called me—I'd given her the details in case Mum ever changed her mind and wanted to see me. So I was there at the end. But she didn't forgive me, Marco.'

'Because she couldn't forgive herself, maybe,'

he said. 'She knew she'd let you down, hadn't looked after you properly. And she'd introduced you to Barney. She'd let him do what he did to you. She couldn't forgive herself for it, and she couldn't tell you that, so she just made you feel that it was your fault—and it *wasn't* your fault, Becca.'

'I wish we'd made up,' she said. 'And it scares me. Maybe there's an alcoholic gene in my family. My mum never said why we never saw my grandparents, but maybe one of them was an alcoholic. So was she. So was I.' She took a deep breath. 'And I always said I'd never get married, never have a family, because I don't want to pass that weakness on.'

'Firstly,' Marco said, 'you're very far from weak. You're strong. Yes, you were supported by the rehab centre, but you were the one who took that first step and asked for help. By sheer determination, you got yourself sorted out and away from all the mess of your life. Secondly, you're not your mother. You wouldn't ever abandon your children, and you'd steer them away from drink and drugs.' He dropped to one knee. 'As for marriage? I hope very much that you'll reconsider that and marry me. Be the perfect modern royal escort.'

'I'm not perfect,' she said.

He smiled. 'Don't you see? That's what

makes you perfect for the job. You're human. You're brave. And you can move on from mistakes you've made. But…'

Her eyes widened. 'But?'

'This is the third time I've asked you, now. If you don't want to get married, then I'll respect that. Provided that you'll live with me. Be my love. Be part of my family. Because I don't ever want to be without you again, Becca. I need you with me. I love you.'

She dragged in a breath. 'But how can your family ever accept me? I'm from the *gutter*.' She shook her head. 'I love you enough to walk away and let you find someone suitable. Someone who'll make you happy.'

'I don't want to find "someone suitable".' He grimaced as he made quote marks with his good hand. 'I want you. You're the one who makes me happy, Becca.'

'You don't have a choice. You're a prince of Sirmontane.'

'I do have a choice. And, before you even start thinking it, no, I don't have to choose between love and duty. I'm free to choose you.'

She couldn't let herself believe it. Dared not let herself hope. 'There's no way your parents will be able to accept a former addict as your partner.'

'Yes, there is.' He sighed. 'Look, come and meet them. Then you'll see for yourself.'

'Meet them?'

'I'm under royal orders to tell you that they want to meet you. Not to be intimidating, but welcoming. Actually, I have a feeling you'll get on incredibly well with my mother. And then,' he said, 'your doubts will all be put to rest and you can do what we both want and agree to marry me.'

He was right—it was the only way she could be sure. Except she was pretty sure that she was the one who had it right, not him.

'OK.'

Marco grabbed his phone from his pocket and called his mother. 'Mamá ? No, she said no. Not until she's met you and Papá. OK. Yes, here would be good. *Talué*. Yes, I love you, too.' He laughed, and put his phone back in his pocket. 'Righty, Ms Anderson. One bluff thoroughly called.'

'Your parents are coming here?' she asked.

'If we go to Regent's Park we'll have to run the gauntlet of the paps.'

'And so,' she pointed out, 'will your parents, if they come here—and that's not fair. We'll go to them.'

'OK. I'll tell them to stay put.' He rolled his eyes and made two more calls. 'All sorted. Rafa says the back entrance is the quieter one, so we'll use that one.'

So much for quiet. The paparazzi were three-deep. Flashlights popped as Marco helped Becca into the car, and there were ribald comments and calls of, 'Are you giving the prince some *special* treatment, Becca?'

She remembered what Declan and Lexi had told her about dealing with the press: be polite, be gracious, and don't let them see that they've got to you. So she just smiled, said nothing, and got in the car.

She felt unbelievably nervous about meeting Marco's family. What if they didn't like her, after all?

Marco, as if guessing how tense she was, simply held her hand. 'It's going to be fine.'

How could he be so sure?

The drive to Regent's Park was over way, way too soon.

But at least Maria the housekeeper was there to meet her with a hug. 'Lovely to see you back, *hermosa*.'

'You, too, Maria.'

'Your parents are in the sitting room,' she told Marco.

'Thank you, Maria. Maybe we could have some coffee in a little while?'

Oh, help, Becca thought. *Please don't let me spill it all over that expensive silk carpet.*

Her nervousness grew exponentially as they walked up the stairs to the next floor and Marco opened the door to the sitting room.

What on earth did you say to the King and Queen of Sirmontane? She should have asked Marco in the car about formal addresses. Too late, now. Hoping that she was doing the right thing, she swept into a low curtsey when they were standing in front of Marco's parents. If a prince was Your Highness, his parents must be the next rung up. What did people call the Queen of England? Hmm… She couldn't call a king 'ma'am', could she? She was just going to have to wing it.

'Good morning, Your Majesties,' she said.

Marco coughed. 'How come you never curtsey to me like that?'

She looked up at him and rolled her eyes. 'Because you don't deserve it.' The words were out before she could stop them.

Oh, no. Why had she said something so *stupid* in front of Marco's mother?

But, to her surprise, Marco's mother burst out laughing. The Queen of Sirmontane stood up and held her arms open. 'Now I know you're definitely the right girl for my son. I did have my doubts.'

Because of the press?

The question must have shown on her face, because the Queen of Sirmontane explained, 'When you curtseyed to us. But, no, you're exactly what he needs. A breath of fresh air. He's absolutely right about you. Welcome, Becca.'

Oh, my God.

She was being offered a hug *by a queen*.

This couldn't possibly be protocol.

But the fact that she was being offered a hug proved that Marco was right, that his family had already accepted her. It made the last barriers of fear round her heart melt. So she stood up and hugged Marco's mother right back.

'Sit down with me, *hermosa*,' Marco's mother said, sitting down herself and patting the seat of the sofa next to her. 'Now, I'm Elena, and this is Alfonso.'

First-name terms with a king and queen.

This didn't seem real.

'Maria's been singing your praises,' said the King—Becca didn't quite yet dare to think of him as Alfonso. 'She says you've helped her a lot.'

That business with her arthritic hip. And Becca had been sworn to secrecy about it. 'I don't want to be rude, Your Majesty, but may I plead patient confidentiality?'

Elena smiled. 'Of course you may. But she's

told us everything. And I'm cross with her for not saying something before, because we could have sent her for treatment much earlier and got her some more help.'

'There's something about this house and extremely stubborn women,' Marco said, lounging back on one of the tall-back chairs and giving his mother an insolent grin.

Elena gave him a speaking look and ignored him. 'So Maria will have more of a supervisory role in future,' she said. 'Thank you for helping her, Becca.'

'It was my pleasure,' Becca said, meaning it.

'And we would like you to know that we would be very happy to welcome you to the family,' the King said.

'Even though...' There wasn't a way to put it tactfully. 'After all the stuff the papers said about my past?' Becca asked.

'The way you've come through adversity would inspire a new generation,' Elena said, surprising her. 'And your example might also give Marianna—Ferdy's fiancée—back some of the confidence that the press has chipped away.'

'I agree,' Alfonso added. 'I think you'll be good for us, Becca. You've made Marco happy. And steadier than he's been in quite a while.'

'I am *here*, you know,' Marco said, sounding pained.

'And we're your parents, so we can talk about you in front of you,' Elena said crisply. 'Always. Even when you're a white-haired grandfather yourself and we're ancient crones.'

Alfonso coughed. 'Since when can men be crones, Elena?'

'You can be an honorary crone, then. Add it to your titles,' Elena said.

Becca couldn't help laughing. She really, really liked Marco's family. And to think that she'd been afraid they'd be stuffy and formal. Lexi had been right about them: they were down-to-earth. Elena was wonderful. Brisk, no-nonsense, and with a rapier-sharp sense of humour. And Marco had been right, too: Becca had the distinct feeling that, in the future, she and Elena would be good friends.

'Now we've got that sorted, I think Becca and I need a quiet chat,' Marco said, and stood up. 'Excuse us, O ancient crones-to-be.' He took Becca's hand and pulled her to her feet. 'We'll be back shortly. Because I am *not* having this conversation in front of you, Mamá.'

'Spoilsport,' his mother grumbled. 'Becca, I want a full report.'

'You'll get it,' Becca promised with a smile.

Marco took Becca up to the roof garden.

'So can you see it, now?' he asked softly.

'That my parents are very happy to accept you in my life.'

She nodded. 'I like your parents. Especially your mum.'

'Mamá,' he said, 'can be a bit full-on. And she's horrendously bossy.' He smiled at her. 'They say that women marry men like their fathers. I guess it's the same for men.'

She looked at him. 'Are you calling me bossy?'

He grinned. 'I love it when you're bossy. But sometimes I want to be the bossy one.' He dropped to one knee. 'Becca, I don't have a ring to offer you right now, because I want the fun of choosing it with you. But will you do me the honour of being my wife, the love of my life and the centre of my family?'

Being the centre of a family. What she'd always secretly wanted and always feared she'd never have.

And, best of all, waking up with Marco every morning, knowing that it would be a good day because he was there and he loved her as much as she loved him.

She knelt down to join him. 'Yes,' she said, and kissed him.

EPILOGUE

One month later

'Ready?' Marco asked Becca.

'Ready.' She smiled at him and stole a kiss. 'My first ever royal engagement. Well, royal-to-be,' she amended.

'It still counts as royal,' Marco said. 'And I can't think of a better place for it,' he added as he helped her out of the car outside the rehab centre.

'Be careful with your arm,' she said. 'You're only just allowed to do medium activities with that hand.'

'Yes, dear,' he teased. 'You can nag me about the exercises later. Stop worrying. I'm fine.'

Thanks to a donation from the royal family of Sirmontane, the rehab unit had been able to set up a new physical therapy room to help their patients.

Cameras flashed as Becca got out of the car.

She waved and smiled at the paparazzi, who'd decided since the news of the engagement broke that she was their darling rather than their demon. Instead of calling her Wild Child Becca and sneering at her, they'd nicknamed her Princess Braveheart and cheered her on.

The fact that at her last press conference she'd spotted that two of the journalists were shaking their writing hand, and taken them to one side and taught them exercises to relieve the pain, had only made them love her more.

Marco was rather less thrilled that the press had also taken to calling him Prince Zorro, but he put up with it for Becca's sake. If she was happy, then his world was all right.

They did the tour of the rehab centre, as agreed—but it took rather longer than planned because Becca stopped to talk with every single one of the young patients. And every single one of them was smiling when she left them, knowing that they were understood rather than judged.

His wife-to-be, Marco thought, was a real shining star.

'I'm delighted to declare the physical therapy room open,' she said, and posed with the oversized scissors in front of the ribbon for the press. Then she smiled and cut the ribbon. 'And may everyone who uses this room find their inner strength, too.'

Like she had.

Marco was so proud of her. She'd come so far. And, just as his parents had predicted, she'd inspired a new generation—across Europe, not just in Sirmontane and England. And politicians finally seemed to be noticing the problem of addiction among teenagers and were setting up more rehab units to help them find their way back.

As they came back to the royal limo, one of the press called, 'Kiss her, Prince Zorro!'

He smiled at Becca. 'I guess that's telling me my royal duty.'

He kissed her, to cheers from the crowd.

'I'd just like you all to know,' he said, 'how proud I am of my Princess Braveheart. And I can't wait to marry her in four months' time.'

In the cathedral next to the palace in Sirmontane where he'd been christened, his parents had been married and his father had been crowned.

He kissed her again. 'I love you, Becca. Now and always.'

She kissed him back. 'And I love you, too.'

* * * * *